REDHEAD ON THE RUN

REBECCA ROYCE

Redhead on the Run (Redheads #1)

Copyright @ 2020 by Rebecca Royce

Ebook ISBN: 978-1-951349-47-9

Print ISBN: 978-1-951349-59-2

Cover art by Lucy Smoke of Smoking Hot Covers

Content Editing: Heather Long

Copy Editing: Jennifer Jones at Bookends Editing

Final Proof Editing: Meghan Leigh Daigle of Bookish Dreams Editing

Formatting: Heather Long

Published by Rebecca Royce

www.rebeccaroyce.com

For Jen Mishkin, just because.

Life can only be understood backwards; but it must be lived forwards.

-- Søren Kierkegaard

CHAPTER ONE

I'd never get used to hearing gossip vloggers talk about me. Did anyone? I held my phone in my hand, watching as they dissected me for public scrutiny. I tried to not get in the way of the people whose job it was to make me look pretty for this blessed occasion.

Pictures of myself in various outfits parading around at important events passed over the screen as the gossip website queen spoke about it in animated tones.

"I'm told that today is the day." She had a little bit of a lisp and squealed on the last syllable of the last word—day. I couldn't decide if her affectations were put on or really a speech impediment that she'd tried to have fixed but hadn't entirely corrected.

Getting that video already uploaded was an impressive feat for Amanda Hill—her name, according to her website. It must have been a slow entertainment day in the world if thousands of people and growing—according to her view count icon in the corner of the screen—viewed her talk about my wedding day.

I was famous, but not *that* famous. It wasn't lost on me

that I added to her number of views this very second by watching it myself.

"One of our four *favorite* redheads is marrying her Prince Charming today. Well, if her version of a Prince Charming has a coke problem. I mean...who does coke these days anyway? It's so passé. At least he has the *princely* bank account."

Again with that squeal on the last word. I shook my head and then stopped when my hair person glared at me. Whoops. Kit's people were going to threaten the gossip site to get that last part down fast. Inside my own head, I rolled my eyes instead of shaking my head at her description of Kit's coke problem. Passé?

Using the word *passé* was so *passé*. It was two in the morning where she was in New York City, since it was eight in the morning in Paris—where I was currently sitting. She must really have wanted this story for her vlog to go out fast. The watch count was up a hundred just since I'd started viewing. I sipped my iced coffee while the woman who was doing my hair talked fast to the woman who was plucking my eyebrows. I'd had all of this done before I left Manhattan, but apparently, we'd missed a spot on my left brow. I should have been grateful they'd found the stray hair. I would certainly read about, hear about, and have to endure having it analyzed over and over online if I looked anything but perfect today. Find the hair. Pluck the hair. Comb the hair.

My best attribute was my red hair. They called my family *the redheads*, after all.

It wasn't like I could really be upset about the hair thing. I was famous for no other reason than I was born into my family and all of us had our late mother's red hair. Being very rich and one of a set of triplets with a notorious father had been enough to garner interest in everything about me since I was born. And before today—my wedding day—it had never irked me.

But it was right now. Big time.

The door flung open, and my future mother-in-law, Laura Allard, strode in, followed by my sisters Hope and Bridget. They were already in their matching bridesmaids' dresses. Well, my sisters were. Not my future mother-in-law. I'd had little say in how this wedding was put together, not even picking out my own dress or the violet ones my sisters wore. Kit's family, led by Laura as a true matriarch, was old money. They had class in a way that we didn't—according to Laura. When I married Kit, one of the things I'd be gaining for my family was a certain Allard cachet we didn't currently have, since Dad had earned his money in investments and not had any growing up.

Well...we'd be getting the old-money reputation that meant we were classy all of a sudden and about thirty billion dollars in estate money Laura and her husband Bill would probably invest in my father's fund of funds very quickly. It was a great merger, sorry marriage, for all of us.

"Turn off that trash." Laura Allard, nee McKinny, took the phone from my hand and set it aside, turning off the app entirely. She'd always treated me like I was beneath her. The whole new money problem. Laura liked to forget that she had no money before she'd gotten pregnant with Kit and forced Bill to marry her, lest they have a scandal on their hands. The woman, who had been his—gasp—secretary before that, had become the filter on who and what was acceptable ever since. She might want to forget her less than auspicious stride into wealth and privilege, but the internet had a long memory and Wikipedia had been my friend when I needed information about her.

Any second now, she was going to launch into her latest speech. The Allards always did this, always did that. I was sick to death of listening to it. Kit assured me the pontificating would end after the wedding—the last thing she would get to dictate. The Allards always got married in Paris, France. This time, it was going to be in Palais Royale followed by a reception on the rooftop of the Hotel Raphael. All of it just small enough that neither family could invite everyone they knew. That was how we kept it exclusive. I'd been to neither place, hadn't even let myself google them to see what they looked like, and paid little attention when we'd marched in here two hours ago to start the process of making me look acceptable. What was the difference? None of this would have been the wedding I would have chosen.

Kit was my choice. I loved him.

I swallowed. Fuck me. Didn't I? I loved him. I did. Right?

I'd met him when I was seventeen but hadn't dated him until I turned twenty, two years ago. That was after a drunken night at a club where he'd confessed to me that he was in love with me. And Kit was gorgeous. Tall, dark haired, with green eyes that a girl could get lost in. I used to, all the time. He could be truly wonderful.

At his heart, Kit was an artist. He painted. Not that he could talk about that very much. Allards weren't painters. No, they were lawyers and business people who didn't particularly go to offices but still had titles and the look of respectability. His father was drunk every day from about two o'clock on after playing golf, badly, every morning. And Kit was going to be exactly the same way after he finished getting his MBA that he would do nothing with.

My body went cold.

"Time to get you in your dress." Laura clapped her hands together and grinned at me. For all that she disapproved of me, she equally loved the idea of me being her daughter-in-law. They'd never had more attention to her so-called charities as she had the last months since Kit put the ring on my finger.

My own truth, what I should have known already, hit me

hard like someone had taken a bat and struck me over the head with it. I. Wasn't. In. Love. With. Christopher "Kit" Allard. Not even a little bit. I couldn't even stand him.

And he pretty much hated me, too.

I laughed, covering my mouth, and all eyes were suddenly focused on me.

"That's funny?" Laura looked from me to my sisters as though they could explain my outburst. How would they do that when I couldn't even speak the words myself?

Hope walked over to me. She and Bridget wore matching up-dos today, which was so strange looking because they'd never let themselves be styled remotely the same, not since they'd had a say in what the nannies laid out for us to wear. I'd liked it, dressing like them. I'd liked it a lot longer than either of them had.

Why was that?

I blinked as Hope took my hand. "Babe? You okay?"

Bridget watched me from two steps behind Hope. That wasn't surprising. Hope was always the first to rush into any situation, while Bridget hung back, observing. If I was involved in whatever was happening, I stayed even further behind Bridget because I never had anything to offer to a situation that was of any value. Hope was kind, talented, smart, and Bridget was all of those things with the added bonus of a compulsive drive for success that matched my father's and then some.

And then there was me. Sweet, quiet, good for the family's image, Layla.

Who was going to marry a guy who hated her—who she equally disdained—because that was the best thing for the family right now. I could contribute nothing else of value to anyone except giving away my body and soul to keep our quarterly numbers up.

I smiled at Hope. This was a familiar feeling. If I

pretended to feel nothing bad, I never did. Why feel bad? I was young. Rich. Gorgeous. After today, I'd get on with getting on. Anything I wanted I'd have. Kit wouldn't care what I did as long as I was discreet, and when it was time for us to have a baby, I was sure Laura would let me know.

"You sure?" Hope squeezed my hand again, pressing at my unspoken answer. She understood what I hadn't said.

We were triplets. We'd shared a womb. Hope and Bridget were my first friends. We'd done everything together, and it used to be because we wanted to and not because my father's PR company told us to be somewhere at a specific time for a photograph. The three redheads. If you added our older brother, four. But Justin was a different story. He'd always been separate, and these days, he was Kit's favorite partner in crime when it came to partying.

The two bored men together.

And now I was going to be sister to one and wife to the other.

The woman who had been plucking my eyebrows—when had she stopped?—held out my dress to me, and I stared at it as I rose from my seat.

"Layla?" Bridget said my name. "Do you need some water or something?"

I shook my head. "No, I don't want to have to pee."

Laura smiled. "Good thinking. I hope you didn't eat anything this morning either. We need to make sure it zips up."

It was going to be fine. I weighed myself twice a day. Once in the morning, once in the evening before dinner so I could judge how much to eat at any time. The scale hadn't moved in the upward direction in the last two years. Down, yes. Up, no. I was always, constantly hungry.

I smiled at Laura. "It'll fit."

The dress was beautiful but not my style. It had been

designed by Daniella Lareine, whose real name was Danielle Gordan. I guessed that wasn't hip enough. She was the 'it' designer of the moment. The Allards wanted to seem trendy while maintaining some tradition by having the wedding in Paris. It was a romantic dress. A-lined. What they would call a sweetheart dress with an open back, except for one piece of fabric that ran down the center of it.

I looked like Cinderella waiting for her prince, just as Amanda Hill had said on her vlog. This would not have been the dress I'd have chosen if I'd been allowed to pick. Not even close to what I'd wear, which was funny because the one thing I'd done in my life, the one real accomplishment I had was a book I'd written about fashion. About getting to your true look. Well, I hadn't written it. I'd had a ghostwriter for that. But I'd dictated information and worked on it.

I knew and understood fashion, how to make people look great in what they had.

I stepped into the dress and nearly fainted as they zipped me. Could a dress feel like a coffin? Was it covered in poison seeping into my skin? Killing me slowly?

I smiled. God, I was so good at playing pretend.

Hope narrowed her gaze. "Something wrong with the dress?"

"No, of course not. This is gorgeous."

"And you look stunning in it." Bridget walked toward me. "But of course, you would. You are so beautiful, Layla. The most beautiful bride there ever was."

I supposed that was something a mother would say to their daughter on their wedding day. Ours had died when we were only a year old. She'd taken one too many sleeping pills and not woken up the next day. Leaving a two-year-old boy and a set of triplets for her emotionless husband to not raise himself. No mother meant Bridget got to play the role today. My father certainly wouldn't.

That was okay. I wasn't marrying a man with no feelings. He had plenty of them, that was why he did so many drugs—so he didn't have to think about any of them at all.

"You look beautiful." It wasn't hard to tell my almost mother-in-law and sisters that. They were gorgeous. In violet, even though I wouldn't have picked the dress, their eyes really popped out. Everyone who said we were practically identical hadn't taken a good look at our eyes. Mine were blue. Hope's were brown, and Bridget's a deep green. Our faces weren't the same either, although we did have the same high cheekbones, and if someone really looked, our red hair wasn't exactly the same either.

I wore mine long, halfway down my back, always had. It was wavy and took a lot of maneuvering to keep it neat looking. Hope had cut hers a long time ago and never had it longer than her shoulders. While Bridget's was long and straight, something I'd envied her for every day when I battled my curls to not frizz.

And just like that, I was dressed. I was ready to become the next Mrs. Allard.

The room was stone dead silent. Was this how it was when others got married? I'd seen movies and pictures where there was champagne and laughter. When was the last time I'd done anything like that? A year? Two? The night that Kit confessed his love?

A knock sounded, and everyone stirred to activity. It was like I was outside my body watching it happen. Laura let Justin enter the room. He fussed over me about how pretty I looked while his eyes remained dead looking, like he'd rehearsed the words over and over until they were meaningless and pointless coming out of his mouth. For just a second, I could actually feel pity for him. When had he died inside? Was there anything I could have done about that? We'd never been what anyone would call close. Justin was like this remote creature we'd shared a gilded cage with for many years but didn't really know.

He handed me a box that Laura took from me immediately. A gift from Kit. It was a diamond tennis bracelet, huge and expensive. Not my style. Laura attached it to my right wrist, fussing over it.

"Layla?" Bridget caught my attention. "Is there anything that you need?"

I shook my head. "Not a thing."

I was doing what I was supposed to be doing. This was my role in my life. I had no other purpose except to fulfill this moment. Flowers were placed in my hands, and I held on to them like they were a lifeline. Walking out into the hall, I took my father's arm. He was steady but not strong. Forty-two years old, but he looked older. Every year, it was like he aged ten.

He didn't tell me I looked beautiful. Didn't remark on me at all. Maybe I wasn't the only one who was going through the motions. Our guests waited around the corner in an outdoor seating area especially made for today. We walked in that direction, no one saying a word.

That was when I saw *him*.

While I should have been looking at Kit, who waited on the other end of the aisle for me to become his wife, I couldn't take my eyes off someone else in the crowd. The whole crowd of people were standing and waiting for me, but he was the tallest person there right now. I might not have seen him right away, but my security team, ever present, had moved and caught my attention in that direction. My father's business partner for the last twenty years, Ezekiel Scott, looked downright bored where he stood.

Amusement flooded me. He was fucking done with this situation, and I didn't have to see anything except the fact that his arms were crossed over his chest like he was waiting in line to get a flu shot rather than attend my wedding.

I'd always been preoccupied with Zeke, the few times in life I'd been allowed to be around him. In their partnership, my father was the trader and Zeke the salesman. He made the deals that let my father do any trading that made them all money. Or at least, that was how it used to work when they'd been amassing their millions. These days, it changed. Something about the fund of funds they were doing now. I didn't really understand much of it, but it seemed there was less for my father to do and a lot more for Zeke to pay attention to.

Dad was always yelling at Zeke, and if the noises I could hear from the phone at the dinners I was forced to attend were any indication, Zeke was always yelling back. They didn't see each other in person and did business mostly remotely with the occasional bitter argument spoken through their cell phones. It was volatile between them. And something about what I was doing today was going to help my father in that situation with Zeke. High finance was like a foreign language to me, and I hadn't asked any questions because it wasn't like I could understand it if I did. I wasn't Hope or Bridget. No one talked to me about real things that mattered.

My heart rate picked up. Zeke was gorgeous in a way that other men just were not. He was four years younger than my dad. Thirty-eight. Dad aged, but Zeke didn't ever seem to. He was somehow more virile than he'd ever been before in that moment as I walked down the aisle. I couldn't even believe he was here. He never came to anything he didn't have to when it came to us. Not birthdays or graduations. He sent checks and someone deposited them for us.

But Kit and I were getting married in Paris, and he lived here. I guessed he didn't have any choice but to attend. How could he get out of being here at my terribly boring wedding when he'd rather be anywhere else?

Movement caught my attention toward the front. Kit was there. He didn't look bored. No, he was sweating, and his hands were shaking. That wasn't nerves. He was coming down from something he'd taken. We were getting married while he was withdrawing. Was I just...fine with that?

When had I become okay with everything being so mediocre?

"No."

The music was loud, too loud. I hated it. Who had picked this song? I didn't want to get married to some traditional bridal march like I was just another marching bridal doll scooting down the happy married walk so we could get on with things.

My father stared at me. We were almost to Kit. Everyone was smiling. Some woman on his side dabbed at her eyes. Why were they crying? Because it was so beautiful, or because they felt so sorry for the two of us since there wasn't an ounce of bravery in either of our bodies?

I hated Kit, but I'd spare him this. I'd do this for the both of us.

I yanked my arm from my father's hold. "No. I can't do this. I'm sorry, Daddy, I just can't."

I must have shouted because despite the timbre of the music blaring like it wanted to bring down the Eiffel Tower, I made myself heard. There were gasps and people started yelling.

"Layla." My father spoke through clenched teeth. "You can't do this to me."

I shook my head. "I'm sorry, Daddy."

"Oh thank God." Hope's voice reached me, but I had no time to consider what she said. I was too busy turning and running down the aisle in the opposite direction. I couldn't think or consider what I'd just done. This was right. It had to be. Kit and I could live in abject misery the rest of our lives, or we could not do this to begin with. I was voting for plan B.

I ran and ran, leaving everyone in my wake. This was problematic. I was never alone, couldn't remember the last time I'd spent any time by myself. I always had at least one security person with me because of some issue Dad had with people who wanted to harm him by getting to us. I didn't even care. No one was going to hurt me. Not if I kept moving and never let myself stop.

I was in Paris, right by the Louvre actually, and I had no idea where I was going. I didn't speak French, not a word of it. Languages didn't work for me, like many other things my brain just couldn't do. In my wedding dress, I didn't have pockets or any money. Not even my cell phone. That didn't matter. Crowds of people waited outside of the Louvre, and I rushed past them.

It had to be a bizarre sight, some redheaded woman running in a wedding dress past tourists in the middle of Paris.

I ran until I lost my shoes. No one stopped me. By contrast, people seemed very happy to get out of my way. Eventually, I felt like I'd actually been running in a circle and not getting anywhere particularly far. I stopped to catch my breath. No one chased me. I was all on my own in the middle of who knew where Paris without a friend in the world. I'd left all of them back at the Palais Royal, what few I had. Most of them were more like acquaintances I did things with when I wasn't seeing Kit that night. Or after I left Kit to go do whatever partying he was going to engage in without me.

I'd had some real friends at the beginning of college, but then I'd dropped out to pursue my fashion career. That was what we'd said to the media. The truth was I couldn't cut it in school. I just wasn't very smart.

Never had been.

I supposed it hadn't mattered very much.

I sat down on a bench. What had I just done? I put my head in my hands. The time to leave Kit was not at our wedding. It was a week ago. A month ago. The day after he proposed. I stared down at my ring he'd given me. It was princess shaped. I hated it. I should have known then. Poor Kit. Oh fuck. What was I going to do?

Thoughts raced but I had no answers for them, so there was nothing to do but sit there and...and what? I didn't even know.

Several cars came to a screeching stop in front of me, and my solitude was over. How long had I sat here? Three minutes. My father. Our security, led by a man named Michael Li, chased after him. My sisters. Justin. They were all there, and all of them started talking all at once, but it was only my father's voice I could hear.

"How could you do this?" he yelled, putting his finger right in my face so close, he grazed the edge of my nose. He'd never hit us. That would have required him to care a lot more than he actually did most of the time. Nannies handled things, and then we went to college. As long as we never ended up in jail, we were pretty much golden with him.

Lately, he'd been downright happy with me. I'd even gotten a smile last night at the rehearsal dinner. But he wasn't happy with me now.

I sucked in a breath. I couldn't even blame him for this. The Allards had planned the wedding, but my dad had paid for it. "I'm sorry, Dad. I was walking down the aisle, and all I could think was that I couldn't possibly go another step toward him. He's not the one. He's not... I'm sorry. I really am. Daddy, I know this was the wrong timing and..."

"The wrong timing?" He laughed. "Do you know how long

I had to work to convince them to let you two get married at all?"

Wait...what? I'd barely digested that when he continued.

"My stupid daughter who will never amount to anything. Marrying Kit was the best thing to ever happen to you. Do you know what this wedding cost? But forget that, do you know what you've ruined?"

Tears that should have probably shown up before now streamed down my face. I wasn't crying for Kit. No, it was because my father was yelling. I'd never been able to abide being screamed at. It was almost automatic for me to weep just from the raised voice alone, forget what they were saying to me altogether.

"You are going to pay me back for this."

I didn't understand. "How am I going to do that?"

"Dad." Bridget sat down next to me, drawing me against her. "Stop it. I'm personally relieved that she didn't marry that asshole. Kit is a piece of shit."

He ignored her. "You have ruined me, and I am done with you. Forget your life. As of this moment, you are cut off. Live, die. I don't care. Your security? Your checking account? It's all over. Layla Radford, you are now the nothing you've always been."

"No," Hope yelled next to him. "You can't do this to her."

The trouble was that he could, and I didn't have a clue what I was going to do.

CHAPTER TWO

"Father." Justin approached. Dad had always preferred him. The son he'd wanted before he got saddled with triplet girls and no wife to raise them. "Maybe we should calm down."

My father threw his head back. "This could ruin me. Calm down. Layla, every cent of this disaster will be on your shoulders until you pay me back. I hope you like that bench. You'll be sleeping on it."

"No, she's not." Hope's cheeks flushed red. "We won't let you do that to her. She'll stay with me or with Bridget. You're not putting her out on the street because she didn't want to marry a man she's not in love with. Kit isn't worth her spit. Not with her kind heart. Just no."

He pointed at Hope and then at Bridget. "If you two interfere in this, then you're cut off, too."

I gasped. No, I wouldn't allow that. Hope and Bridget were worth ten of me. They were smart, brilliant. I wouldn't take away their opportunities. No, that couldn't happen.

"I'm sure we can work this out." Justin smiled, a tight lifting of his cheeks.

"The only way this works out is if she comes back to me on her knees begging. And even then, she'll pay back every cent she owes me for this farce. You're on your own, Layla. I'm done with you. Your credit cards are closed. I'm taking my money out of your bank account. We'll call it paying off your tab." With a long look he glared at my siblings. "You have five minutes to say your goodbyes. Or you're done, too."

He stormed into his car, leaving Michael Li to stand there staring at us. His people had guarded us for almost a decade. Although my father had declared himself done with me, it would seem Michael wasn't quite sure what to do. Did he leave us there or go with my father? His gaze halted on the bench, and he changed his stance, broadening how he took up space in the world. I guessed he didn't mean to leave.

I rubbed at my face. This was just like me. I made a rash decision, and now everyone was going to suffer. This was going to be exactly like the time I'd wanted to sneak out to go see that concert in Central Park and we'd all been grounded because of it. No, I could do better this time.

"You guys need to go."

Bridget shook her head. "We're not leaving you here on this bench to be homeless. He can go…suck a duck."

I stared at her a long second before Hope and I both cracked up. Suck a duck? English was our first—and in my case only—language, but sometimes, I could hear our nannies in her expressions. That one was one of our first nannies. Her name had been Nadia, and she'd lived with us when we temporarily resided in Monaco. That had been the years Dad had been looking for a better tax haven. I hadn't understood that then. I'd just thought it was stunningly beautiful, and I'd loved the views from my bedroom every morning.

Nadia used to say that. I put my head in my hands, laughter fleeing abruptly. "You've worked too hard to do this. I'll go beg. That's what he wants, that's what he'll get."

"You'll do no such thing." Justin knelt down in front of me. "If you do that, there is no coming back from it. Trust me. But we're not just going to leave you here, either." Justin rubbed his nose. His eyes were red. I knew this look well from Kit. My former fiancé had taught me the signs well, and even in the midst of this personal crisis, I couldn't help but have my heart clench as I stared at my big brother. When had it gotten this bad? Justin slipped something into my hand. "That is my debit card. Use it to take a taxi to the Hotel des Oiseaux."

Hope scrunched up her nose. "Birds. The hotel of birds?"

He waved his hand at her. "It's very exclusive, and she'll see when she gets there... Yes, there are birds. Never mind that right now. It's in the seventh arrondissement. You'll be fine if you get there and wait for me." He rose. "In the meantime, you two go back to the hotel where her stuff is and retrieve it before he thinks to have it thrown out. Her cell phone. Her wallet. They're probably at the venue where she was dressing, but the passport will be at the hotel. Hurry about it."

Bridget jumped up. "I'm going to have to ride in the car with him to go do that."

"We all are." Justin sighed. "If we don't go with him, he'll find a way to make this even harder on her."

I couldn't believe my brother was taking control like this. It was so not like him to do this. Justin was always pretty removed emotionally from whatever was happening with all of us. "Layla, wait for us to leave. Get a taxi and meet me there. I'll take care of you. Okay?"

I wiped at my eyes. That was so nice of him, so unexpected. Bridget shook her head at me. She didn't understand it either. Next to me, Hope squeezed my shoulder. "We'll take care of everything and meet you there."

"Thank you." I wiped my eyes again.

Justin put out his hand. "I'll take the ring."

Maybe my head was just too fogged up after everything, but I had no idea what he was talking about. "The ring?"

"On your finger. You left Kit at the altar. You're going to need to return that. I'll do it for you."

He was right. I did need to return the ring. Fuck. I hadn't thought anything about that. With shaking hands from the adrenaline in my system, I pulled the ring off my finger and handed it to Justin. When he would have pulled his hand away, I held it there. "Hold on. This, too."

The tennis bracelet Kit had given me needed to be returned to him as well. He stared at the bracelet for a long moment before he closed his hand around the diamonds I'd placed there. "I wish things were different, Layla. Please remember that."

"You're helping me so much. Thank you." I'd really never be able to show Justin how much I appreciated this.

Hope shifted in her seat. "Right. Very surprising, big brother."

"Come on." He nodded toward the car. "Just get to the hotel."

Kissing my cheek, Hope smiled. "We'll fix it."

I didn't think things could really be made better. But I wasn't being abandoned by my siblings, and that was a gift I'd never be able to repay. Bridget furrowed her brow, a string of her red hair falling into her eyes. She stared intently at our brother. I wished I could read her mind like twins and triplets could do in stories, but if anyone had that talent, it hadn't been me.

They walked past Michael and headed into the car. The head of security looked at me and then the car. He stalked over to me and leaned down. "It's safe right now. We don't have any immediate threats to be concerned with. But I don't like leaving you, so try and fix this thing with your father soon. Okay?"

I think that might have been the most he'd ever said to me in one moment. He'd always been impressively quiet. I nodded. "Okay. Thanks."

Maybe everything would be okay.

My optimism lasted as I watched the limo drive away, leaving me on a bench in a country where I couldn't understand a word the locals said. I even managed to find myself a taxi. It had been years since I'd been in one. If I wasn't in a car being driven by paid staff, I used ride shares. But since I didn't have my phone, I couldn't do any of that, and so a taxi was my only choice.

I'd taken French in school. We'd all had to, and I'd lived in French-speaking countries, but I couldn't speak or understand any of it. I'd never been able to. It was just another way that my brain perpetually failed me. Any language other than English eluded me, no matter what I tried to do about it. The taxi driver must have understood me enough to get me to the hotel. We pulled up to the building, and I let out the breath I felt like I'd been holding the entire time.

The cab driver spoke, and I knew enough about life in general to understand that he wanted to be paid. That was sort of universal. I handed him Justin's debit card, gratitude flooding me that he'd given it to me.

He was going to meet me here, and everything was going to be fine. I'd never have believed it, but my brother was actually coming through for me. All the years that he'd tortured or ignored me were behind us. When I needed him, drugs or no drugs, Justin was there.

The cab driver said something else I didn't understand and shook his head wildly. I stared at him. Something was wrong. He held up the card and repeated the same phrases plus some new ones that didn't sound any nicer as he pushed the debit card in front of my eyes.

It took me a moment to realize the card hadn't worked. That was impossible. There had to be something electronically wrong. Justin's card would be good. He'd never hand me a means to pay for this taxi that was going to be denied.

Would he?

"I...I don't have anything else." Not a thing, and that wasn't an exaggeration. Panic crept up my spine. What in the hell was I going to do? "Can you try the card again?"

We went back and forth like that for a good long time. Over and over, he'd try the card, it would be rejected, and he'd yell louder at me. That didn't make what he was saying any clearer. Was he going to call the police? Was I going to spend the night in a prison in Paris? What was going to happen here? I...

The door flung open and standing in front of me was Zeke Scott, my father's business partner. My mouth fell open. What was he doing here?

He regarded me for a second before he turned his attention to the cab driver, saying things back to him that I also couldn't make out before he handed him some cash. At least that stopped the shouting.

Zeke reached in and grabbed my arm, basically yanking me out of the cab a second before the disgruntled driver took off like a bat out of hell down the block and away from where we stood watching. Gentler than he'd tugged me, Zeke let go of my arm.

"Sorry about that. I was half-convinced he was going to abscond with you as some sort of interest payment."

That was a really stupid joke, but I laughed because I was so fucking relieved, I could hardly contain myself. "Wh— what are you doing here?"

Why was it hard to breathe? Someone had to have called him. This wasn't just random. It couldn't have been...

"Hope called." He held up his phone. "Asked me to come get you, that you'd be arriving in a taxi you couldn't pay for."

My sister had saved me. "Why didn't the card work? What is going on?"

"Seems that your brother has taken off with some diamonds that you gave him. He and Kit took the money and ran, so to speak." He shook his head. "Stupid idiots. At least he sent you here. I happened to be here. I don't know that I'd have crossed town to save you somewhere else."

Okay. I was cooked. Fried. The dress that had earlier felt like a coffin was now like a noose. There was nothing around my neck, and yet it felt like someone choked me to death. Had all the air been sucked out around us?

Zeke placed his hand on my shoulder. "Layla. Do us both a favor and don't pass out. I'm really not in the mood to play any bigger role in your drama today than the one I've just been forced to manage."

My panic shifted from anxiety to anger in two seconds flat. "In my what?"

"Don't shout either. The entire world doesn't need to hear our conversation."

My day really couldn't get much worse. I'd run from Kit and left him at the altar. My father hated me, my brother stranded me at a hotel with no money, and despite his promises to come, he was obviously not going to do so. And Hope had sent Zeke Scott to get me—the man of my teenage fantasies—and he was proving himself to be just another asshole in the long line of men that I knew in this world.

I took a long breath. It didn't really steady me, but I was going to pretend that it had. "Where is Hope?"

He looked away for a second before practically glaring at

me. "On an airplane with Bridget and your father. They weren't given the opportunity to get your stuff."

That wasn't possible. Justin, yes, he would abandon me, but not Hope. She and Bridget never would. I was one hundred percent sure about that.

"Hope said to tell you," he pulled out his phone and stared down at it, "that she had no choice but to get on the plane. They drove straight to it, and if she doesn't get on it, things will be worse for you. She will explain when you two next talk."

I was fucked. I closed my eyes. I was in Paris. I couldn't speak or understand a word being said to me, and I had almost no money in the account that was mine. My brother had stranded me at this hotel. What was I going to do? I counted to ten. It didn't help. I was going to have to fake my way through this.

When I lifted my lids, I'd pulled it together at least well enough that I wasn't going to cry. I hoped. "Zeke." I didn't know that I'd ever said his name aloud before. I'd said it plenty in the dark when I was all alone and imagining things I'd want done to my body. Asshole he might be, but gorgeous nonetheless. Besides, if today showed anything, it was that I had no sense whatsoever when it came to choosing men. Even my fantasies proved to be bad for me.

He lifted his eyebrows. We stood under a covering that led into the hotel. If we turned left, we'd be inside, right would take us back to the street. "Layla?"

That was twice now he'd said my name. It was a new record. "I need a minute. I...I don't know what to do, and I have to think. My mind...it doesn't want to work at the moment."

"Does it work at other times?" He shook his head.

That was it. My father had been done with me, and I was officially done with this conversation. What had I done to

Zeke to deserve this? I'd not even asked him to come and rescue me from the cab. Had I hit his dog with my car and didn't remember? Injured him in some way that earned me his disdain?

"What is your problem?" He didn't want me to yell, but that was what I was doing now. "I'm sorry you were inconvenienced. I realize this whole morning has probably been a lot of boring for you, but my life is falling apart, and I would appreciate it, given that you are a family friend, if you could try to be a little less rude."

My lower lip trembled. It was a telltale sign I was going to lose it. Full on sobs were on their way if I didn't suck this back in. I hated crying. Not that anyone ever liked it. But it wasn't like I had a whole lot of experience with anyone taking care of me when I cried. I was mostly told to knock it off.

"Do you want me to pat your head and tell you it's all going to be okay? You ran out on your wedding and pissed off your father, little girl. What did you think was going to happen?"

I boiled over. He'd done me the favor of igniting my temper. It at least made the tears vanish. "I'm not a little girl. I am obviously a grown up, and I don't want you to pat me on the head. All I asked you to do was to give me a fucking minute to think."

He shook his head. "You're a grown up? You could have fooled me. The most immature twenty-two-year-old I've ever met. Went from living off your father to being ready to live off your husband. The bravest thing you ever did was run from your wedding, and now here you are, a sniveling toddler. I thought you might finally have grown a backbone when you booked it away from Kit, but here you are, still pathetic. You disgust me, Layla."

I smacked him, hard. Nothing had ever felt better.

But reality quickly rushed back in. I'd just hit my father's business partner, and he was the only person who could possibly help me, given my situation.

There was no rule book for what to do here, no articles I'd ever read on how to handle a man I'd just whacked for being rude to me on the worst day of my life. I lifted up my chin. Yes, at some point, I was going to fall apart. No, it wouldn't be in front of him.

"Apologies." I nodded. "We can be done with whatever this moment is and never see each other again."

For his part, Zeke was beautiful in his anger. Men shouldn't be so completely beautiful to look at. Tall, broad shouldered. He wore his perfectly tailored blue pinstriped suit. It didn't wear him. He'd been using the same watch for as long as I remembered, and he never took it off, no matter what the rest of his outfit happened to be. When I needed to catalog people, I always did it by starting with their accessories. I'd done it since I was a young child. Small details and then outward.

His face was sculpted like he'd been made to be photographed. These days, he wore a neatly trimmed brown beard and the hair was thick on top of his head, begging to be touched. His eyes were dark, brown, and endless in their depths, even though they were so angry. I couldn't blame him. One side of his face was bright red from where I'd struck him. I'd not been gentle about it.

"Thank you for saving me with the cab."

There I'd officially said everything I should say, and now I was going to hightail it out of here and try to find my way back to my hotel, where I presumably had a room until tomorrow and where my stuff was currently stored. Unless my brother had ransacked that, too, although I wasn't sure how he could in the time we'd been away from each other. Considering traffic, it was amazing my father had gotten to the airport so fast. But then again, he did seem to make the world move to his liking.

Goosebumps broke out on my arms. I could do this. Somehow.

"Layla." Zeke's voice was lower this time when he spoke. I'd struck him, and I knew very little about him. Was he going to be the kind of guy who hit me back? I'd never had that happen. But I'd hit him and...

He nodded towards the hotel. "Let's get you a drink at the bar. And then we'll go get your stuff from wherever it is."

I blinked. What had he just said? "A drink?"

"That's right. You've had a long day and it's only lunchtime. Well, almost lunchtime. It seems like the kind of day that deserves a drink, even as early as this."

I rubbed my arms. "I just hit you."

"I'm aware." He still hadn't rubbed his cheek. "Come on. Drink."

I walked toward him. My feet were starting to ache. I had no shoes, and I was pretty sure when I looked at my feet later, they were going to be cut to pieces. Every step shot agony up my legs. The good news was my dress was so long, no one could see I was shoeless. Small wins, I supposed. "Why are you taking me for a drink when I just hit you?"

"Because I deserved it, and I can't remember the last time someone so perfectly gave me what I deserved." He walked ahead of me, letting the doorman open the doors for us as we entered. I was getting a lot of looks from bystanders and pedestrians. A wedding dress now covered in dirt and mud with my hair half falling in my face was naturally getting me a lot of second glances. If they happened to know who I was, then it was going to garner me even more attention.

Zeke took my elbow, drawing me to him. "But don't make a habit of it, Layla. One hit, yes. Two, and I might think you're telling me you want me to hit you back," he whispered in my ear. "On your ass." I almost stumbled, and he stopped me from falling. "Maybe you do."

I didn't know what to do with any of this. "I..."

Whatever I would have said, I didn't manage because I was suddenly struck by the beauty of the hotel I'd just walked into with Zeke. My brother had said it was the hotel of the birds, and that was what it was. Marble representations of doves and some other representations I didn't recognize were everywhere. It should have been cheesy, but it absolutely was not. It was beautiful. Someone had taken a lot of time to carve and display those birds. They were everywhere, and I couldn't get enough of looking at them. The details were extraordinary. All-consuming and astoundingly beautiful.

"You like them?" Zeke stopped so I could look around.

"They're... Yes, I like them. They're beautiful."

He smiled at me. The first time I'd ever seen him do that. "I do too. Some people don't. Some people make fun of the birds, but I feel like there's nowhere on Earth I could go other than Paris that I could see this."

The rest of the hotel was equally as striking, or at least the bit I could see on our way to the bar, which was right off the lobby. The lighting changed immediately upon entering the space. It was darker inside, with burgundy walls that had gray panels all around the space. A fireplace wasn't lit but evident in the corner, with a gold screen that contrasted with the silver everywhere else. A giant mirror showed the other side of the bar, displayed over the fireplace.

For the early part of the day, it was fairly busy inside of the bar. Three bartenders rushed up and down it, clearly busy, but all waved at Zeke as he entered like he was an old friend.

It begged the question, "Do you come here a lot?"

"Yes." His answer didn't give me a lot of information, but I supposed he'd told me what I'd asked.

We sat down, which was hard in my dress, and almost

instantly, one of the bartenders was right by our side. He spoke to Zeke, and they conversed back and forth without me having a clue what was being said. Eventually, they both turned and stared at me. I had no idea what they wanted.

Zeke leaned back in his seat. "What do you want to drink?"

"I'm not much of a drinker. I don't know..."

The bartender spoke again. I smiled but had no idea what he wanted from me. Eventually, Zeke looked back at me. "You don't speak a word of French, do you?"

I shook my head. "Not one."

"Okay. I'll order for you. He speaks English, but he doesn't like to. Might be easier if you don't have a preference if I just did it."

I nodded. "Sure. You order."

That was the easiest choice I'd made today.

"How do you not speak French? I thought you four went to the best schools wherever you were living."

He wasn't wrong about that. We had. My father didn't want us in boarding school, for whatever reason he'd never shared it, but we always attended really good private schools wherever we happened to have moved. He didn't like to settle, or stay anywhere too long. Once we were astronomically wealthy, we seemed to up and go even more than we had when we'd been only extremely rich.

"I'm not very smart." People, when they noticed the things I couldn't do, and they did notice, didn't tend to remark on them. It was the whole I was richer than they were thing. But when they did, that answer seemed to shut them up fast.

Zeke tilted his head just slightly. "That's obviously not true. Despite a lack of judgment, maturity, and common sense, you are able to converse, seem to have a high vocabulary, and I've heard you speak on videos that our PR department sent me. You are obviously smart enough."

I remembered those videos. I didn't work for the company doing anything substantial, but I did have some title in the charitable giving department that Hope ran. That was how I got my health insurance taken care of. That was gone now, too. So much for my birth control. Another thing I was going to have to figure out. Or I'd just refrain from having sex. That would be the best idea. No sex, ever again. I didn't like it that much anyway. Better to just take care of myself. Only I was capable of giving myself an orgasm.

"Layla? Still with me? Not going into some kind of dramatic shock where you'll have to be locked away to heal from your ordeal?"

My attention was right back on him. The bartender returned with two drinks. A champagne looking cocktail for me and a whisky for Zeke. He took his straight up, not even ice to filter away any of the intensity of the drink. I'd never been able to stomach whisky, it was just too much, so I supposed I should feel lucky he hadn't ordered that for me.

"Sip if you haven't eaten anything. I'm not going to hold your hair for you. In fact, we should get you some food." He spoke to the waiter again who ran off quickly.

I lifted my drink to my lips. It was sweet and obviously had champagne in it, as the bubbles tickled my tongue. Other than that, I wasn't sure what I was drinking, and at the moment, I couldn't seem to bring myself to care.

"So, you don't speak French because you're not smart." He lifted an eyebrow and set down his drink. "You left Kit at the altar for...reasons. I really don't want to hear about them. Your father has cut you off. Your brother stole from you and abandoned you in a country where, as we've already determined, you can't speak the language. Your sisters have left, for reasons I'm inclined to believe that they had no choice about because Hope seemed frantic. But in any case, you are alone."

I took a longer sip of the drink. "Yep, that's pretty much it."

The waiter set down some peanuts in front of me. I supposed it was a good thing I wasn't allergic. Still, my stomach turned at the idea of eating. I set my drink aside. If I couldn't eat, I wasn't going to continue with the alcohol. Justin used substances to not have to deal, I didn't.

"After this drink, I'll take you to get your stuff and then we'll figure it out from there. I can put you on a plane to New York if that is what you want."

That made the most sense. I should go home. I had an apartment that was paid for until the end of the month when I was supposed to move in to live with Kit. So, I'd lose that soon, but at least it could take care of me now while I figured out what to do next. Hope and Bridget both had rooms I'm sure they'd let me crash in until I...until I what? I had no earthly idea. But I just had to do the next right thing. One step after another. Then the future would show itself to me.

Fuck me, I sounded like a self-help book in my own head, and even I knew it was bullshit.

"Thanks." I had no other choices, nowhere else to go currently.

He nodded. "You're welcome."

Zeke brought the glass to his mouth and sipped the whisky. I watched him, hoping he didn't realize I was staring, but that action might have been the most sensual thing I'd ever seen. He met my gaze, and I had a feeling he knew exactly the direction of my thoughts. Zeke probably had women staring at him all the time, because he was like a walking advertisement for sex. They could probably sell bottles of that whisky here if they just sat him in this chair and instructed him to sip it all day.

Well...a walking advertisement for what sex was supposed to be and not what it was. Movie sex. Imaginary sex.

"If it means anything, I think Kit and his entire family are crooks. I think they're bad people. Maybe not Kit. I don't know him. Why would I? But his parents? Yes, particularly the mother. You're well rid of them."

I ate a peanut. It was warm, salted, with some other spice on that. What was it? I loved it. I ate another. Then another. Food really was better in France. Not that I got to eat very much of it. I had to watch my weight, but I could eat the entire bowl of these peanuts. The thought made me push them away. Anything I liked too much I had to get rid of, at least when it came to things with caloric intake.

Did my run through the streets count as my daily cardio?

"Thank you." I finally responded to his speech about the Allards. I couldn't say I disagreed with him. "But my father may never forgive me. He needed the money they were going to give him the second we got married. Well, you know, you work with him."

Instead of answering me, he took a long sip of his whisky. "Remind me how much it was?"

Shouldn't he have known that? "Don't you know?"

Warning bells were going off in my head. I tended to listen to them. When you grew up like we did, you learned when someone wanted something from you. I tended to know almost instantly, and I was really good at quickly figuring out exactly what that was. I was many things, but naïve wasn't one of them.

He set down his drink. "No, I don't unfortunately, because your father has been, for some time now, hiding money and information from me. Things I need to successfully and honestly put an end to a partnership we should long since have dissolved. But he's hiding money. So, I can't do that, because I'm not going to be cheated. Not by him. Not again."

CHAPTER THREE

W ell...I'd give it to him. Zeke hadn't lied or pretended that he knew something he didn't know. That was slightly...refreshing.

"Again?"

He shook his head, a scowl coming across his face. "Your father is one of the most unscrupulous, untrustworthy, terrible people I've ever encountered in my life. And I've known a lot of bad people." Zeke looked away for a second. "I made him a very rich man, and to be fair, he made that, too. But I'd give it back to never have known him. I could have made someone else, someone less...pitiful. How much money was he going to get from the Allards? Something I suspected, by the way, but couldn't prove."

I suddenly felt like I was being asked to divulge state secrets. People didn't talk to me about things because they didn't think I'd understand, and most of the time, I didn't. But sometimes they spoke in front of me for the same reason, like I was so stupid I couldn't hear them or grasp their meaning, even sitting there in front of them. Like I was a decoration left on the mantle, placed and soon forgotten.

My father had just thrown me away like I'd fallen and broken. He'd had me forever but was happy to discard me, like I'd never mattered at all. I was taking this metaphor too far, but that was how truly wired my mind was at this moment.

Who was I betraying? No one. They'd cared so little about what I did and didn't know that no one had bothered to tell me it was a secret to begin with. "Thirty billion dollars."

My answer must have been rather significant, because Zeke took the longest sip of his drink, yet. "I see. And do you know where he was going to put that money?"

"That goes beyond me. I'm afraid they'd never have mentioned that to me."

He sat forward. "Who would know? Hope? Bridget?"

"Yes, likely they would know."

It was like I could see a plan forming in his eyes. I'd spent a lot of time studying him, but I had no idea exactly what he was thinking. I just knew this was about to turn the day on its axis, again. How many times could a day do that?

"And I don't imagine you could just ask them. That would be too obvious, they'd guard up, and besides, you're not going to betray your sisters since they are the only people who give a shit about you at all."

My stomach burned, and my bravado threatened to flee. No. I wasn't going to go back to almost crying. That was too hard, too miserable. "Thanks for that." I let sarcasm drip from my tone. It wasn't like me to do that, at least not aloud. But he'd earned it. "Yes, I'm luckier than most to have that much love in my life."

"Love is overrated. I've never believed in it. Why bother?" He rose. "But I'm wondering if keeping you would just be enough."

"Keeping me? Enough for what?"

He got to his feet. "Come on. Let's go get your stuff. I don't think I'm putting you on a plane tonight or any night soon. That is unless you want to go back to people who don't care if you're there or not."

I rose slowly. The dress was constricting, my feet hurt, but my mind was whirling. It was like we'd hit that wall where everyone else was going to understand what was happening except for me. I had to tread slowly to not make some kind of mistake.

"What are you saying to me?"

He put out his hand. "Right this second, I'm saying we're going to go get your stuff. Unless you'd rather stay here not eating peanuts or drinking your drink."

A woman rushed over to him, throwing her arms around him before kissing his cheeks one at a time, in the way that was so un-American and so French to do. Also Italian, Portuguese, and other places I'd lost count of. Her arrival startled me. It had seemed a little bit like we were alone in a cocoon, he and I. Sure, the waiter had come and gone, but it was like the rest of the world couldn't really intrude on us here.

That had been ridiculous. I barely knew this man, and the leggy blonde who had moved from kissing his cheeks to trying to kiss his mouth certainly did. She'd have succeeded, but he set her aside in a swift move that was impressive in as much as anything because it indicated he'd done it before.

Throwing her a smile that looked fake to me, he spoke to her in French. Well, I assumed it was French. I really couldn't hear the difference.

She turned to me, and her eyes widened. After she said several things, I was actually able to make out the word Layla. Great. She recognized me. Looking like this. Next, she'd be taking a picture. Or wanting a selfie.

"It is you." She spoke to me in English. "I didn't believe

it." Her accent was light. Whoever this beautiful woman who wanted to kiss Zeke was, she spoke nearly flawless in English. I never ceased to be impressed that people could do that. "I said to myself, it couldn't be the redhead with Zeke. Why would Zeke be with the redhead?"

Depending on who I was talking to, people either called me the redhead or one of the three. I did have a line I used in response that I said so much it really had become just that, a line I said like an actor delivering a speech. "Oh, I'm hardly the redhead. If you looked about here, I'm sure you would find two or three more. We're rare but not that rare."

She smiled. "Oh, you are adorable even in this...wedding dress?"

Zeke took my hand. The act startled me, and I stared at our joined fingers. It wasn't as though we had some kind of history where we did that sort of thing. He'd tugged me around quite a bit, actually, and I couldn't say I minded. What did that say about me? Something bad? Something good? But holding my hand was different. More intimate, somehow?

"Sophie, yes, this is Layla Radford. We have to go."

She stared at our joined hands. "Oh, I see. Yes, you have to go." She laughed. "I obviously see the attraction, Layla. We've all seen the attraction, but you know our Zeke. He doesn't ever have just one of us."

No, I hadn't known that. I was digesting that information when Zeke must have had enough. "Good to see you, Sophie. We're leaving."

"Layla," she called after us as we hustled out of the bar. "I would love to go shopping with you. You will make me look like my best me, yes?"

"Um, sure, if we can do that." I was trying to be polite. I had to be whenever someone approached me. Every person on the planet had a platform to talk about me if they wanted one. They could post and post and post. Enough people started to say that I was a spoiled, entitled bitch, and eventually, that would be what I was whether it was true or not. I made sure that I was always kind, always polite, always someone they thought might be their best friend if given enough time.

And my security always made sure they didn't get the chance to be too close for too long. I guessed that Zeke took that role now since I no longer had any. They'd not really been with me for me anyway, more like to prevent me from being kidnapped so that my father could be forced to pay ransom for me. I didn't guess he'd pay that now.

My feet hurt, and I wasn't going to be able to keep up with him much longer like this. "Zeke, I don't have any shoes on."

He stopped, looking me up and down for a second. "Really? What happened to your shoes? Or were you always barefoot?"

"I lost them in the run. My feet hurt and..."

He ran a hand through his hair. "Fuck." A second later, he'd scooped me up and strode out of the hotel holding me like he was going to carry me over a threshold. It was sort of funny. I was in a wedding dress, and he was carrying me around like something out of a movie.

Only I didn't know him, this wasn't that, and I had no idea where he was taking me.

"We're going to the car," he answered my unasked question. "And then I'm going to take you to your hotel room to get you some shoes, collect your stuff, and we'll go from there."

I held up two fingers. "That's how many stops we have to make."

"Right, I'd known that. We have to go back to that venue, too. Fine. In the meantime, I want you to consider staying."

Oh, we were back to this. The moment right before Sophie had shown up when I was confused and didn't know what was going on. I was still in that zone. What was happening here? "How could I do that? I have no money."

"You don't need it. You'll be my guest."

Being carried like this might have been the most awkward conversation position in the history of all conversation positions. "Why would you do that? We don't know each other, and I have the distinct feeling that you don't like me very much."

"I don't like anyone that much. People in general. Maybe because I understand them too well after a lifetime of selling them on things they probably shouldn't be doing. Trust me, if I can make bank executives invest in your father's crummy platforms, I can make anyone do anything. I'm leveling with you. Keeping you will make your father crazy. He will fume over this, and it will give me the ability to finally figure him out with his guard down. Or he'll make a mistake."

He opened a car door in the parking lot. It was a two-door Porsche. I'd been in a lot of them in my life. I knew men cared a lot about this kind of thing. I shouldn't be genderizing. Some men and some women probably did, too. Hell, I needed to keep my head focused. When he would have strapped me in, I stopped him. There were some basic things I was absolutely capable of doing for myself.

Zeke shut the door and went around to the other side. With traffic so constantly bad in Paris, I couldn't imagine he got to open this up around town very much. But it was probably more about having it than actually driving it. There was status to this car, and it probably got girls like Sophie to agree never to be exclusive with him.

"What do you think?" He started the car.

"About what? You haven't really told me anything. You

want to make my father nuts by keeping me. Is that what you want me to help you do? Stay here and make him nuts?"

He drummed his fingers on the steering wheel while he pulled the car out into traffic. It was the middle of the day, and it was going to start to rain. My reception would have been ruined. I smiled. That was sort of funny. It would have been a terrible disappointment to everyone. They hadn't put out the tents. And rain had not been in the forecast.

"I can help you. What I saw today when you booked it away from your chosen life partner was a person who needs to take some control of her life. I can help you do that. By the time you go back to New York, you can have some say over your destiny. Trust me. I pulled myself out of a shit hole. I pulled your father out, and I can help you do the same."

It sounded lovely. But too good to be true was too good to be true. "That would make you just like my dad. He paid for me, too."

"By the time I'm done with you, you won't need anyone else for that the rest of your life. Layla, you can be the captain of your own destiny. Then no one can touch you. Ever. Trust me on that. You'll say when, who, and how. The world can fuck itself if you tell it to. You won't have to ask your father or your sisters or anyone for help. I'll help you. If you help me. A little quid pro quo."

I sat up straighter in my seat. "Really?"

"Really." He nodded. "You help me, and I'll see to it that you will never have to run from anyone ever again. They'll run from you, honey. I promise you that."

CHAPTER FOUR

W as it possible to even consider this? That was the question that plagued my mind the whole drive over to the hotel. I'd limped into the hotel behind him, declining to be carried because that was just too much. Once, okay, he'd surprised me, but now he'd put it out there that he wanted to *Pygmalion* me into some kind of woman who could take on the world.

It turned out my bags were packed and waiting by the front desk for me. The staff ran fast, holding all of them out to me as soon as I came through the door.

Zeke spoke to them in French before turning back to me. "You have a passport in the safe, right?"

Yes, as it turned out, I did. "How did you think of that?"

"People put their passports in the safes in their rooms. We all do that. It's not rocket science. They cleaned up your room because Laura Allard told them to. But they didn't get the passport, so let's go do that now and get it out." He gave some more instructions, and suddenly, my bags were being brought outside. I watched them go a little bit like I was watching a television program I'd just stumbled upon. There was a distance to everything, the sense that nothing was real, even though it was happening.

Maybe my adrenaline was crashing.

I followed Zeke and the manager, who was really talking fast, into the elevator and headed back upstairs to the room I'd exited that morning before sunrise. A guest entered on the next floor before we continued on to the fourteenth floor where my room had been. Who had picked this hotel for us? This wasn't where we were supposed to have gotten married or where our reception would have been. Why had we stayed here?

The second the woman in the elevator recognized me, her demeanor changed. She was tall and maybe thirty years old. She was in a bathrobe, so she was either coming from the spa or the pool. I assumed there were both those things in this hotel. I supposed it was possible she just liked to walk around in her bathrobe. Stranger things had happened.

"You're Layla. One of the redheads." Her accent was British.

I put on my smile. "I am. But I mean, there are lots of redheads. I bet you can find three or four others here. We're—"

"My God," Zeke groaned behind me, leaning on the elevator wall. "Really? Every time?"

I ignored him. He could go suck on an egg. "Sorry, he can't control himself. We don't pay attention to him, and you shouldn't either." I smiled broader at the woman, hoping she'd remember that and not Zeke's outburst.

"Oh, I would love to shop with you." She practically squealed. "And you can make me look like the best me."

I nodded. "I'd love to be able to do that if we had the time." The elevator dinged. "Have a wonderful day."

I limped out of the elevator, letting everyone else walk in front of me in the hall. While the manager did that, Zeke didn't. He glared at me as he slowed his stride to match my own. "Do you give that little speech every time someone knows you, and what is that thing they keep saying to you? Look like the best me."

"I wrote a book. That was what I talked about in the book. Helping people to dress to look like the best them."

He lifted his eyebrows. I'd surprised him, and I couldn't imagine that happened very often. "You wrote a book?"

Here was where I could lie, except I never did. The thing about a ghostwriter was that I didn't have to tell anyone I'd done that. Only I always had. In every interview, every conversation ever, I'd admitted to it. I hadn't really written the book, not technically.

"I didn't write it. I collaborated on it. I can't write a book. I'm not smart. I'm not able to do things like that. But I talked to the woman who wrote it, and she wrote it trying to be as close to my voice as she could possibly be."

He nodded. "Lots of famous people do that. Not everyone is able to sit at the computer and... You know what? How many times a day do you say that I'm-not-smart thing?"

We'd gotten to my room. The manager opened it, and I walked in, going straight to the safe. I always used the same code, so it was no problem getting in there to pull out my passport and my wallet. I held both in my hands, turning myself back to Zeke. I was sure the manager could speak English. I'd never stayed at a hotel where most of the staff couldn't speak the languages of the guests, at least well enough to communicate basic things.

But if he weren't embarrassed, I wouldn't be. "I don't say it that often, actually. Most of the people I talk to on a regular basis know already."

"Okay. That's the last time you'll say it. Consider me informed of your opinion on the subject. I don't want to hear it again."

I shook my head. "You asked, so I had to explain."

"Fine."

We rode in silence back to the lobby. Zeke was stewing about what I'd said, or maybe it was something else I did. Or maybe he was just angry about the shape of the elevator. I'd never imagined him so moody. The manager practically bowed to him on our way out, and I limped my way into the car.

Sighing, I waited for Zeke to come in the other side, and when he didn't, I turned around to see what was going on. He was in the trunk, digging through my bags.

"What the hell?" I pushed open the door. "What are you doing?"

"Socks. Shoes. Do you own any that aren't high heels? Do you own socks?"

I gritted my teeth. "I do own sneakers. I didn't pack the bag. That was some stranger my would-have-been mother-in-law paid to do, so for all I know they've been stolen."

"No." He pulled them out and strode over, carrying a white pair of socks with him. He knelt down in front of me. "Give me your feet."

That was sweet, and I almost laughed before I stopped myself. This man didn't give the impression that he was particularly gentle and kind all that often. "I know I'm not smart." I said it purposefully to piss him off. "But I can put on my own clothing."

He narrowed his gaze. "Fine."

Although I was sure he wanted to throw them at me, he instead handed them to me gently and stormed to the other side of the car. Twice now, I'd provoked him, and twice now, he'd not really reacted in a terribly mean way.

Sure, he probably had a line he couldn't be pushed past, but I'd hit him, and he hadn't done anything about that at all.

Who was this man who tried to put my shoes on, buckle my seatbelt, and had no qualms about yelling at me in public?

Why didn't he know the rules about dealing with me? You never did anything you didn't want to see later on five different social media platforms.

Or did he just not care?

As he drove his Porsche through traffic, I examined my feet. They were torn up, and much as I was glad to have my shoes to put on, I almost didn't want to touch them. They needed to soak before I even attempted to put shoes back on.

"Stay in the car," Zeke said as he pulled into a space.

I should have argued, but the truth was that I didn't want to. If he wanted to be this nice to me, my sore feet were going to take him up on the offer. He left the car running, and I watched from behind the tinted window as people stared at it on their way into the hotel. Most of our guests from the wedding-that-wasn't were staying at the reception site, and I was glad I didn't have to go there to collect anything.

It would be very awkward to have to see my ex-fiancé's great aunt right at this moment. Zeke was back fast holding a trash bag I presumed held my stuff in it. Laura Allard had certainly been busy getting my stuff removed from everywhere I'd been. Even the hotel room that should have been mine until the next day.

Zeke got back in the car and held out my phone to me, which I gladly took. He must have pulled it out of the bag. The trash bag got shoved in the small area in the back, that wasn't really a seat but could hold a bag of that size. Thank goodness I hadn't had very much stuff here. Had it only been hours ago that I'd been here getting ready to get married?

He didn't speak when he drove away this time, and I looked down at my phone to distract me from thinking about how all the plans I'd had before today were in three bags, including one made for trash, traveling in Zeke's car right now.

My phone had blown up. It was really amazing how many of my friends wanted to sympathize with me and claimed to hate Kit when they'd all been singing his praises the last time I'd seen them. And most of them were already leaving Paris. It was also amazing how much privilege we really had. I hardly ever thought about it. I mean, I knew I'd been rich. Right now, I was as poor as I could imagine being financially, even as I sat in a car with a billionaire. But they'd all been in Paris, and now that my wedding wasn't happening, they'd hightailed it out like I'd asked them to come to some bug-infested nightmare instead of a city people dreamed of seeing their whole lives.

In any case, no one was particularly asking to speak to me. It was like an obligatory text they'd sent to say they did. As I was about to fall off the face of the Earth for most of them, I was sure this would be the last time I heard from at least three-quarters of them. I should have done better than this in picking people to spend my life with. They were just on to the next event, the next photograph opportunity. Did Hope and Bridget have friends? Did Justin?

My betraying brother...

I steadied myself as I opened up Instagram and was immediately bombarded with pictures of myself running away from my wedding. That hadn't taken long. Hell, probably some of the people who texted me were the ones who'd uploaded these shots.

"Everything okay?" Zeke asked without looking at me, which I appreciated. Right then, I needed to pretend I was in a bubble that no one could see through. My own private bubble that no one could see through but me.

I nodded. "Yep."

"Uh-huh." He made a left turn and had a little space

ahead of him, so he revved the engine and we sped up like we were floating in air instead of the road. I should have been impressed. Like my friends should have felt lucky to be in Paris. All of us were really just fucked in the head. Did anything impress Zeke? I wasn't going to ask him. He might ask me back, and then I'd have to explain just how pitiful I was, even in my own head.

"Where are we going?" I should at least know that. Now that I had my clothes, I'd really like to take off this dress. Take it off and burn it. Never have to look at it again. Pretend this whole thing had never happened. That I'd never said yes to Kit to begin with.

"Home."

That was sort of impossible since that was technically in New York City, right? "Can this baby fly?"

He smiled, a real one, like he'd given to me when I'd admired the birds in the hotel. "No. I wish. Funny, I thought when I was a kid, we'd have flying cars by now. But how would we handle that with the air travel? We'd have to book passages in our own cars to not conflict with airlines, otherwise there could be crashes. We'd get in each other's lanes. Can you imagine that noise? The ones that they hear in the cockpits when another plane is even nearby?"

The loud alarm that sounded. He'd clearly been in a private plane where he could hear that noise in a cockpit, as I had more than once. Commercial planes didn't let the passengers hear that. "They'd have to do something about that noise. It would have to be another signal. Like a flashing red light."

"No, it would have to wake you because you'd have to set the car on auto fly for most of the trip over the Atlantic." His smile hadn't faded, and I sort of loved that we were talking about this. It might have been the strangest conversation of my life. Cars didn't fly, and we didn't need to worry about being woken over the Atlantic. But...it was fun to think about.

"I wouldn't sleep. I never sleep on planes. It's like total hell the whole time. But I don't drive cars, so I doubt they'd let me drive one that flew."

He shot me a look, side-eyeing me the whole time. "You're not going to say it, right?"

"Say what?"

Zeke rolled his eyes. "That you're not smart enough to drive a car."

I laughed. It wasn't funny. But the way he said it like it was the most absurd thing he could think of added some amusement that might not otherwise have been there. "I've had no reason to drive. I was chauffeured or we lived in a city where no one drove."

"Didn't matter what city I was living in, I drove." He shook his head. "Driving is one of the great pleasures of life."

"Maybe in a car like this one."

We turned a corner, and he slowed down. This was the first time I got a look at Zeke's mansion. It caught my breath. Maybe I'd been wrong when I thought I wasn't impressed with displays of wealth. I'd seen some of the biggest, most expensive homes and apartments in the world. Sailed on yachts. But I'd never seen anything like Zeke's home in Paris.

I sat up straighter. "Wow."

He smiled. "I wanted a place I could love and that also told certain members of the world to go fuck itself, that I was richer than they were."

"Well, goal achieved."

We'd lived in a lot of places, moving every one to two years it seemed. Perhaps it really would have made sense for my father to place us in boarding school and leave the four of us there. Maybe it would have given us stability. Maybe if I could have stayed in the same place long enough, a teacher or two might have helped me with my learning issues. Or maybe that was wishful thinking. There might not be help for me in that way. Moving hadn't held back Hope or Bridget.

We parked in a detached garage and walked through a white guard house that would presumably keep unwanted people away from entering if Zeke didn't want them to. A guard wearing all black nodded to us, and Zeke stopped to speak to him. I heard my name, but the rest of what he said was lost on me.

Still in my wedding dress, I probably looked a sight. Or maybe they were used to Zeke bringing home strangely dressed women. I still held my shoes in one hand, and I'd slipped the socks into them, one each so they wouldn't get lost. I had my cell phone in my other hand.

"Zeke?" I interrupted him, sorry to have to do so since I couldn't follow the conversation and didn't know if it was a poorly timed moment. "Can you open up the car so I can get my bags?"

He shook his head. "I'll get someone to bring it in. Come on, let's go inside. I was just getting you on the approved list so you can come and go as you wish, since you'll be staying here."

I didn't know that we'd actually settled that. "Am I?"

"Obviously, I'm not going to force you, but I think after we talk, you'll want to."

I followed him onto a cobblestone path that led to the house, white like the guardhouse. It was funny about security. Or maybe funny wasn't the right word. Odd...perhaps. Most people didn't have to go through life living with security. My father did. Zeke did. Arguably, Zeke seemed to have less of it than my dad, who had to be followed around by his. And because of the threats against him, his children did, too. Well, three of them did. I no longer had any.

They got so rich, that they had to employ people to help

keep both them and their stuff safe all the time. Was there some kind of middle ground? Enough money to feel flush with it, but not have to worry that they were going to constantly be robbed?

There was another gate that could be locked behind us, but it looked more decorative than useful. It wouldn't actually stop anyone from busting through should they want to.

Everything was white on the outside of the house except the windows and the painted black lanterns that were probably, I imagined, actually electric lights designed to look old. It really would be weird if someone had to come out and light a flame in them every night. In fact, that would be ridiculous. Oh, the places my mind went. Small details didn't matter, I really had to focus on bigger things. But then all I could see was that there were eighteen windows and they were spotless. Not a stain on them. Not a smudge that I could see, and, thanks to corrective eye surgery, I had great vision.

There might be more. I strained my head back to look at the roof. I was pretty sure there were some windows up there, too.

"What are you looking at?" Zeke stood next to me as he asked me the question.

"Windows." I shrugged. "I like details."

I turned left and stared at the side of the house. It was shaped like an L so I could actually see the whole area if I wanted to and...

"Come on. You can see them from the inside. They work both ways." He winked at me.

Was he teasing me? I wasn't good when people did that, because I couldn't really tell if they were making fun or if they were being nice or some combo of both. Rather than say the wrong thing, I stayed silent. It tended to work in most circumstances if I just stayed that way.

But I almost lost my silence when I stepped inside. There

was never a time that Zeke didn't look perfectly dressed. Fashionable and tailored, but never overdone. I couldn't say the same for the inside of his house.

It was such an odd display. Not everyone knew how to style homes, and I was certainly not an expert and wouldn't claim to be. We'd never lived anywhere long enough to own furniture for any length of time. We'd arrive at a new house, and it would be a whole new set of things for us to use and get used to just in time to go again. It was almost like we were criminals—always fleeing the chance that we might get settled somewhere. Being accustomed to some place was illegal in our world.

But Zeke clearly thought that because he lived in this huge French mansion he had to decorate it like he was in the Palace of Versailles. Gold chandeliers. Persian rugs covering marble flooring everywhere. It was cold on my feet, which didn't feel good under the circumstance. It was almost as though the cold burned.

I limped after him, keeping my decorative opinions to myself. Room after room didn't change my impression, which of course begged the question as to whether it actually wasn't him who had done it. No, this was a decorator. In fact, with their long, heavy drapes and fabric striped couches I saw displayed here and there, I would bet that no one ever came in these rooms at all. He lived here, but he didn't really *live* here.

Chandeliers everywhere. And my god, mirrors. This was ugly. Really, truly, a lesson in what not to do when decorating.

I'd never been so glad to get upstairs as I was when that finally happened. The bedroom he led me to seemed much more like a hotel room than a statement in the history of the French monarchy that the downstairs had been.

"This can be your room." It was the first time he'd spoken in a long time, and I was glad for the noise.

A man I'd not met rushed past us, putting my bags—the garbage bag and two thrown together suitcases—down in front of me.

"Thank you," I said, and he nodded to me.

"Layla, this is Carel. He works for me with three other people. They know you're going to be staying with me for a while, and they're going to do their best to speak to you in English."

Carel cleared his throat. "We're glad to have you. My sister follows you."

I smiled at him. "Thank you for helping me."

He nodded and left. Zeke stood, watching me. "I didn't realize today how famous you are. I guess I knew it, but I'd never focused on it. And having spoken to you today more than I ever have, you're different than I would have imagined. Different from your sisters."

I didn't have the wherewithal right then to ask him in what ways I was different. I pretty much knew the answers. He'd worked with Hope and Bridget. He'd know how... I wasn't even going there in my mind at the moment. I couldn't. There was only so much self-flagellation I could take in one day. And it was... I looked at my phone. Only just about mid-day.

"I'm going to take myself into that bathroom and soak my feet before I wash off the rest of today."

He put his hands in his jacket pockets. "Sounds like a good plan. I'll order some food for dinner. I don't assume you'll want to go out."

I absolutely didn't. "We should talk about why you want me here, but before we do that, I have to ask you a favor." And I hated having to do it like I hated pretty much everything right now.

"What's that?" He lifted his dark eyebrows. Even knowing that he'd hired a terrible decorator to do up his house like some kind of monstrosity out of a horror movie, he was still absolutely the most physically beautiful man I'd ever seen.

I made myself look away, knowing that my cheeks were going to get really red in the way that happened to redheads. "I need you to get me out of my wedding dress. I can't do it myself."

He cleared his throat. "Get you out of the dress? Like undo the buttons and what not?"

"Frankly, I don't care if you take scissors to it and slice it into strips that you then use to wash your windows. But I need to get out of this, and I can't do it myself."

One more humiliation on a day filled with them.

CHAPTER FIVE

He stepped toward me. "Turn around."

I pivoted, grabbing on to the top of my dress in front so that it didn't fall down. "Do you see the buttons?" I'd been so out of it when they'd been putting me in it that I hadn't focused on how long it had taken the woman who buttoned me in to do it. Not long, I didn't think. But she'd been a stylist. They were amazingly adept at all things clothes.

The dress vibrated slightly as he undid one button and then another. There were probably about fifty of them for him to undo. He had big, strong hands with thick fingers. This might be hard for him, but he didn't say a word of complaint.

"What would you have done when you wanted to get out of it after the wedding?"

I smiled. "Kit would have had to have done it."

He was quiet for a long moment before he spoke again, in a low voice. "He'd never have been able to do this."

I pictured Kit's shaking hands. "No, he wouldn't have.

Long night, I guess. Or I'd have had to call someone in the hotel to help me."

"Or sleep, live, eat, and die in this dress for the rest of your life."

This was like the flying car conversation. I liked when he did that. The idea that his mind sometimes fled from the present to the absurd like my own did was fun. And not something I ever imagined when I was touching myself and thinking of his hands on me. My cheeks heated up at the memory.

"Right," I managed to get out. "Or I'd have to stay in this horrendous dress for the rest of my life."

He finished and stepped back. I held on to the dress to keep it over my body and turned to look at him. "I thought you were a fashion person. Why do you hate your own dress?"

"I'm not a fashion person. Not really. Not a designer or a stylist. I wrote, or sort of wrote, a book that helped people to feel better in their own styles, in their own clothes. This wasn't my idea. I didn't even pick it out."

Zeke must have been done with this conversation because he turned and left, stopping only when he was by the door. "I think you have everything you need here. But if you're missing something, let me know. I've never had anyone stay here before, so it's possible something was forgotten. I'm down the hall. Burgundy doors. Knock if you need me."

I limped into the bathroom. We had to have some serious conversations about what exactly he expected for this night, or nights, I got to spend in his house. First, however, I was going to soak my fucking feet. The bathroom was huge with a cast iron tub that called my name. I dropped my dress onto the ground in between the bed and the bathroom and made a limping beeline to the tub, where I ran the hot water. I should put my whole body into it, but for now, it just had to be my feet.

Very rarely did I think about my feet, but when they hurt, they were all I could think about. I tucked myself into the side of the tub to sit on the edge and put my feet beneath the water. I wished it felt wonderful, but they stung, and I was pretty sure I was going to have to clean them off with antiseptic and antibacterial and everything anti before I bandaged them in a few minutes.

I closed my eyes. I just had to breathe. But then my phone rang.

I stared down at it as Hope's name appeared on the screen. I answered it. "Hope?"

The sound of the airplane hit me before she answered. "Layla?"

I smiled. It was ridiculously nice to hear her voice. "What happened?"

"I'll tell you, hold on." She paused for a second. "He's being ridiculously mean right now." Of course, she meant Dad. "And I'm hiding in the bathroom. Bridget is distracting him with numbers."

I could practically picture it like I was there. I'd have been sitting with my legs up, staring out the window or trying to read because I hated airplanes so acutely, I could never rest, and Dad would have no need to talk to me.

"How are you?" she asked again after a long pause.

I swallowed. "My feet hurt."

That wasn't what she was asking me, and I knew it. But it was about all I could get out right then. Everything else was too much. Much as I adored my sister, I wasn't sure she'd understand that. Or Bridget, if she'd been on the phone. I was the only one in the family outside of Justin who might be too lost to count at this point. Maybe I was, too.

Was I?

"Where are you?" Her voice wavered. She was upset. I mentally kicked myself for doing that to her. I'm sure it had been a terribly long day for her, too. And she had to put up with Dad.

I looked around. "In Zeke's guest room bathroom. Soaking my feet. Seriously, Hope, they hurt like hell."

She ignored my comments about my feet. "You're in Zeke's house? When I called him, I thought he would help you, put you on a plane back to us, not take you in. I've never heard of anyone being in that house. Is it huge?"

I made a hmm sound in my throat that I hoped she interpreted as yes. I didn't want to talk about his house, although I stored away in my mind the piece of information she'd just given me about no one coming here. Zeke said no one stayed here, but I didn't know that meant he'd never had guests at all.

Of course, that might not be accurate. He didn't have my family over. That didn't mean people like the woman in the hotel who had wanted him right then and there hadn't been. I shook my head. I was talking on the phone. I needed to focus.

"Yes, he took me home." I should tell her what he'd said about Dad betraying him, about wanting something from me, except I didn't. I chewed on my lip and considered why I wasn't announcing what I knew right this second. Truth was I had no idea. Maybe because I'd been abandoned on a park bench.

I forced my mouth to work. "I'm not sure what happens next. I have all my stuff. I'm soaking my feet. What happened, Hope? Why are you and Bridget on a plane? And fuck, Justin. He... Well, I guess you know what he did." I let myself say what I didn't even want to think, let alone vocalize. "I wouldn't have left you here."

Her voice hitched and guilt assaulted me again. Why did I always feel like I couldn't make them upset? In what way had

I been reared to believe making my sisters upset was the worst thing I could possibly do?

Hope's tears became my tears. I could hear her cry, and so I cried too. Was it all triplets, or was I the worst codependent person on the planet? It would be easier to talk to Bridget. She never cried. Not since we were children.

"Dad lost his mind. He ranted and raved the whole way to the airport. He was saying very weird things. I mean... I understand the business the way we all do." I didn't, but I wouldn't get into that at the moment. "But he was saying things, and suddenly he seemed like he might have a heart attack. I was terrified to leave him. Justin got out of the car at the airport and told us what he'd done right before he took off. I was terrified, not sure what to do. And then I thought of Zeke. Dad said that if we didn't get on the plane, he was cutting us all out. Justin ran off. I...I panicked. I don't know what I'd do if I didn't..."

I stopped listening. I actually understood. Plus, she thought Zeke would put me on a plane. Very little muss, very little fuss. She'd have helped me back in New York City. Hope wasn't abandoning me.

And Bridget would have just trusted Hope to handle it because that was what Hope did. Guilt weighed on my shoulders. "Hope, you didn't make me do what I did today. And you sent Zeke for me. I'm sorry I just...emotionally bashed you."

She laughed, and I was able to take a deep breath again. "I'm so glad you didn't marry that man. I hated Kit the second I met him. He's not good for you. Doesn't see you for all your beauty on the inside. I don't know anyone who gives and gives the way that you do and expects nothing in return."

I closed my eyes. "That's not me. That's Mother Theresa."

"Oh, Layla. Hold on a second." There was noise in the

background. "Sorry, listen, they're asking us to sit. I love you. Come home tomorrow. I'll come and be with you. Until we get this all sorted out. I know we can fix things with Dad."

That was the thing. I didn't want to sort things with Dad. Not anymore. Maybe not again. "I love you."

I disconnected the call and managed to take off my undergarments without too much pain before I lowered myself into the water. The next time I ran from a wedding, I was going to make sure I was wearing sneakers. I let my hand hang over the side of the bathtub so my phone didn't get wet. With a sigh, since I felt about two hundred years old, I leaned my head back and tried to relax. My poor feet were throbbing.

Or better yet, if I ever had another wedding—and sitting where I was now, I doubted that would ever happen because I was going to be paying my father back for this one for the rest of my life—I was going to go barefoot on the beach. With a car waiting to whisk me away right next to the sand should I have to make a run for it.

The tears I'd been holding back, sometimes well, sometimes not so well, since the drink at the hotel, flooded my eyes. I'd blame Hope for this. Her tears had brought my own. Even as I thought that, I knew that wasn't true, but I wasn't good at handling emotions. I'd had no examples on how to do so in my life.

My mother certainly hadn't managed hers very well.

I pushed that away, way back in my mind. I wasn't her. I'd been proving that my whole life.

When the water went cold to match the frozen direction of my thoughts, I pulled myself out of the tub. The towels had been laid out nearby, and I grabbed one. Considering he never had guests in here, the house must be in a constant state of ready just in case someone showed up. They must open the rooms every day, air them out, make sure everything was clean. It was quite an undertaking, but it must have been worth it to Zeke.

A house that was instantly ready to house a stranded woman with nowhere to go.

It was time to doctor my feet. I winced at the thought. This was going to hurt, big time, but lately, most things did. I got to it.

My phone dinged as two messages came through, and although I was quasi-dripping and really uncomfortable, I picked it up to look at it because I was basically leashed to the thing, and I had no idea what to do about that.

Bridget: *Just heard you're at Zeke's. Wow! That's like getting invited to the Batcave.*

I doubted I would find him somewhere beneath the house inventing materials to go eliminate the Joker somewhere in Paris. That was a sweet thought, though. He would look seriously gorgeous in all black, running about in the night saving lives. Bridget couldn't know what her remark would do to me. My crush on Zeke was a secret I'd take to my grave. If my sisters had men they fantasized about, I didn't know about that either.

She was trying to be funny.

But my humor fled the second I saw the next message.

Justin: *I'm sorry, Layla. I'm really fucked up.*

I stared at it for a second before I set my phone down on the counter. I didn't have the slightest idea what to do with that. Was he sorry? And what difference did it make if he was? I knew next to nothing about addiction. Could I really be angry at him if this weren't the least bit his fault but something out of his control?

My own reflection caught my attention. There I was. Everyone said I was so beautiful. I'd always thought out of the three of us that Hope was the prettiest. Her curves were more pronounced than my own. Although Bridget had the most expressive eyes. It didn't matter. Right there was the commodity I brought to the family. My face. My hair. The fact that, according to the PR people at my dad's company, the camera seemed to love me.

What was it that Justin brought? He was the male. The one who had been expected to carry on my father's legacy. His son. He'd been the bright light, the man with the destiny. And now he was apologizing to me over a text message for stealing from me and leaving me in a foreign country with no way to pay for myself.

I couldn't even bring myself to be angry at him because it was just so sad.

Well, I hoped wherever he and Kit had run off to, they were happy with their choices. But that reminded me. I had my own apology to make, and it was a big one.

I dialed Kit's number and listened to it ring. He didn't answer, and I hadn't expected him to. I'd done a shit thing to him, even if it were the right choice to make. He at least deserved to tell me off personally and not over a text message.

"Hey, it's me. Listen, I suspect you know why I did what I did today, but that doesn't make it okay. If I hurt you, I am so sorry. I know I must have embarrassed you, and your family has to be through the roof angry with me. I need to tell you how sorry I am about any pain you are having. And that I wish you well. When you feel like talking, even if it's to yell at me, call and I'll answer."

I almost said I love you. That was habit for me to say to Kit. He said it to me, too. How terrible were we that we said that to each other and neither of us meant it? Did anyone mean it when they said it anymore?

Were they worthless words?

I dried off my hair and limped over to my bag to find my hairdryer. I had no idea how long I'd be staying here, or if I'd be here at all, which meant I wasn't going to unpack more than I had to. This would be the first time I ever did that in my life. Even when I stayed in a hotel room one night, I put away my clothes in drawers. I liked things orderly and where they were supposed to go.

But since I didn't even know where I was supposed to go, that seemed pointless at the moment.

I'd packed for two nights in Paris and an entire trip to Bali, where we were going to stay at a resort on the beach. My honeymoon I'd gotten to pick. The idea seemed sort of ridiculous now. Kit and I had never spent as much time together as we would have on that trip. What would we even have talked about? There was always something in life to do to separate us, and break up the time so I didn't have to notice how little we had in common.

He had calls to make—business, purportedly, but truthfully, I had no idea what he did on the phone. Meetings to take. Again, it seemed so completely ridiculous. It wasn't like he really worked. I'd had photo shoots to go to. Interviews to give. Parties that I was expected to attend. Lunches where I pretended to eat.

What in the hell would we have discussed for a week in Bali?

Would we have talked at all or spent the whole time on our phones avoiding each other in between really boring bouts of obligatory sex? Thank goodness we'd used a condom every time. Neither of us had ever suggested going bare. Maybe we'd both somehow known it really wasn't going to be forever.

I dressed in a casual blue sundress I'd planned to wear to lunch at the resort and put on my sneakers to go with it. No one would be talking to me about fashion choices if they saw me looking like this.

Maybe I should go walk around like this purposefully...

That wasn't helpful thinking.

My inner cheerleader, the one who had been quiet lately, needed to reemerge and fast. I was pretty much blowing up my life without her. Or maybe it was just the opposite. Maybe she had been my inner enabler.

Zeke's house was quiet, and as I made my way out of the room, I realized that I wasn't exactly sure which room was his. He'd said down the hall. Burgundy doors. There were four places that looked like that.

All right. If I were Zeke's private spot in the house, where would I be? I went to the one on the other end of the hallway and knocked. It was as far from me as he could be, and if I were a person who never had houseguests but got saddled with me, that is where I would go.

"Come in," his voice answered, and I opened the door to go in, stopping abruptly as I entered. The rest of the house was ugly as sin, but this room was beautiful. This one really was Zeke's. Dark colors, wooden panels. A bed bathed in black and gold. Low lighting with huge windows that gave the impression the room was lit up by Paris alone.

And standing next to one of those windows was Zeke. Shirtless. Gorgeous. Built out of stone. So handsome, he stole my ability to speak.

In his hand was a shirt that he quickly put on as he eyed me silently. "You okay?"

I wasn't the only one who had bathed and now looked more casual. Zeke was in jeans. I wasn't sure I'd ever seen him in jeans before. They were dark denim, and he'd now dressed himself in a white T-shirt that fit close to his muscles, showing off just how buff he was, a fact I could one hundred percent attest to, having just seen it first hand with the shirt off.

Still waiting for me to answer him, he walked over to the dresser and put on his watch. His hair was slightly damp,

REDHEAD ON THE RUN

and the room had the scent of a shower around it, like he'd left the bathroom door open and the smell of his shampoo and soap had seeped in, making everything seem clean and fresh.

I swallowed. "We need to talk about what's happening."

His smile was surprising. "Can you? Speak, that is?"

I shook my head. "Often and quite well."

"Good. I wasn't sure there for a second if I was going to need to call a doctor." He strode past me. "Come on. You must be hungry."

I wasn't actually, but I followed him from the room. "I'm okay. You don't need to worry about that."

"How can you not be hungry? Rather than ordering, since I wasn't sure what you'd want to eat, I asked Paul to make us some sandwiches and leave them in the fridge. That was pretty universal, I thought. You can bet there is an egg on those sandwiches. I have always loved how the French do that, they just add eggs to things."

Did they? I usually thought about cheese. And café au lait. I did love coffee. "Really, I don't eat at this time of day."

"You didn't eat anything but a few peanuts this morning. You'll eat now."

Okay. I would. "Can we talk while we do that? You can tell me what you want in exchange for whatever you're offering."

"Yes, we can talk between bites. People have been doing it for as long as I can remember. Chatting as they consume sustenance." The kitchen he brought us into was big, well-furnished, and modern looking. Like his bedroom, it seemed a place that was actually used in the house instead of displayed.

He opened the fridge and pulled two sandwiches out. I didn't see any staff. I was sure they were around, but they kept themselves away from Zeke. Where did they spend the day? We'd had help in the house, but none of them stayed very long. Two years at a time. Then we'd up and move again. But none of them hid from us.

Zeke pulled out a chair and pointed at it. I sat down, assuming that was what he wanted. He took the one across from me and placed a plate down that I figured was mine.

"See?" He winked. "An egg."

I could see that. This wasn't exactly a croque monsieur, I didn't think. It was more like just swiss cheese. An egg. Lettuce. And some kind of mustard. I took a bite and discovered there were also little baby pickles embedded in the bread. I wouldn't have thought I'd love it, but it was savory, fresh, and practically exploded in my mouth when I chewed.

"You like it." He took a bigger bite than the one I'd been nibbling on, his gaze not leaving mine as he ate his own. "I didn't ask you if you had any food issues or allergies. I know a lot of people are gluten free or dairy free."

That was true. "No, I'm not any of those things." I didn't have trouble eating any food or any medical issues that would require me to abstain from anything. I just made it a rule to not eat very much. The bare minimum to get me through. I took another bite. This one bigger. What was it about this food that was so much better than anything I'd ever eaten before? The bread? French women were always so gorgeous and thin. How did they eat like this and stay so fit?

Before I'd realized, I'd eaten an entire half of the sandwich. Okay. That was enough. I put my hands in my lap.

Zeke rose from his side of the counter and crossed to a small fridge on the other side of the room. He came back with a bottle of wine that he quickly opened with a corkscrew he pulled from a drawer. Zeke was a person who knew his way around his own kitchen.

"I don't think I should drink. I had one earlier"

He waved his hand. "Barely touched any in the bar. You

don't have to if you don't want to. But it's red wine. You're in France. Have just a little."

He poured two glasses.

"Well, what the hell. It's my wedding day." I laughed. "That calls for drinks, right?"

CHAPTER SIX

"There are always reasons to celebrate. Maybe we both can after today." He handed me the glass, and I took it. Someone else might drink the wine in one big gulp. Zeke hadn't poured very much. But I wasn't that type, even if I wanted to be. I took a sip and then set it down. I knew from too much experience that chugging anything would make me sick. I had what a nanny had once called a delicate disposition.

The drama wouldn't be worth the discomfort.

"You can't possibly be done eating."

I smiled. "Thank you. I am."

He picked up the other half of my sandwich. "Are you sure?"

Zeke held it out to me as though he might feed it to me. That should have been a ridiculous thing. I wasn't a child who needed to be fed. And yet...I found myself transfixed, staring at his big fingers holding that sandwich out to me like he was gifting me the food. All I had to do was take it.

I could say no. He wouldn't shove the food in my mouth or choke me. I lifted my gaze to meet his own. There was a question in it. Would I take it from him? That's what he wanted, to feed me, and just in that moment, although I'd never be able to explain why exactly, I wanted to please him.

I leaned forward just an inch and took a bite from the sandwich he offered me. It was the same savory, amazing taste as before, and yet it was so much more, too. Maybe it was the one sip of the wine. Maybe it was just the few more moments the mustard had been allowed to absorb into the bread. Maybe it was the fact that Zeke held it.

But, fuck, I loved it.

He leaned slightly forward. We hadn't dropped our gazes since we'd held them. I was chewing, he was watching. It should have been uncomfortable. It wasn't.

I was so sick of *should*.

"Another." He lifted his eyebrows slowly. It was like an unasked question. Would I do it? Yes, I would. I took another bite. The slightest smile played on his lips. This was a different one than I'd ever seen him do before.

"Your father is stealing a lot of money from me. As I briefly explained before, half of everything he earns is mine and vice versa. I've kept my end of the bargain, even when I would have preferred otherwise. I wouldn't have made that deal if I'd known what would come. I could have made anyone as rich as I made your father. And someone else would lose and make a fortune over and over again in as brutal a way as your dad did."

I sipped my wine. No one had ever told me any of this. "He lost his money?"

"Over and over again. Stupid, poorly judged market moves. I used to wonder if he'd been possessed by a three-year-old who had never read a market report." He held up his hand like he was stopping himself from saying anything else. "He could have gotten out of this brutal work marriage anytime he wanted to, just by letting me out of it. But he kept us both stuck, and now he's hiding money. So he can start up without me. Part of me thinks I should just let him. We're both brutally rich. I don't need more, and I can finally take my talents and go elsewhere with them. But..." He rubbed his eyes. "Fuck me. I don't have it in me to lose. Not like that. Not to him. Not while he thinks he got away with something."

I took a much longer sip of my drink. Zeke held up my sandwich, and I bit into it, chewing and swallowing.

I'd finished the sandwich. I didn't even realize I had. I'd absolutely eaten the whole thing and hadn't even realized. I picked up my wine glass. It was like some sort of shield between me and the rest of this conversation I was about to have.

"I'm not sure how I can help you with that. You have the wrong sister in your house. I'm the one who couldn't find the accounts or anything. I mean, that's all virtual, right? Can't you hire someone to hack him or something?"

Even one day earlier, I couldn't have imagined suggesting that someone do that to my father. Today? I really couldn't seem to bring myself to care. Did that make me a terrible person? Was that something I should be worried about?

"I have people on that. What I need is for him to slip up. When he gets frazzled, he makes poor decisions. One more bad one, and he's going to have to go get money from somewhere. When he does that, I will have him."

I was finally catching on. "Somehow, I'm going to make him make a poor decision? I bet he has already. Hope said she thought he was going to have a heart attack. I think I've done what you wanted without even knowing."

The wine tasted fierce. It burned a little bit and had a kick to it, like it might lash out and destroy the drinker if given the chance. I'd drunk almost all of it now and wouldn't mind more if he poured it.

Zeke grabbed the bottle and put more in the glass. "You did. You threw him right off his game, and today, our numbers tanked. I lost millions of dollars."

I was so confused. Why was this good news? "I'm...I'm sorry...."

"No, it's a good thing. I need to lose to win. Now, I just need him to get upset again. One more time, and he'll get caught in the web he forced me to spin."

I cleared my throat. "What am I supposed to do? I mean...I left Kit at the altar. I'm not sure what else I could pull off this week."

"Be seen with me. Let's take lots of photos together. Start speculation. I checked out your social media presence while you were soaking your feet." When he said it like that, I felt like I was Nana. She'd died when I was ten, but I could distinctly remember she used to talk about soaking her feet all of the time. I was twenty-two, and I suddenly had that in common with my grandmother. I tried and failed to restrain my grin.

He stopped talking. "Is something funny?"

"You wouldn't get it. My mind is weird. Go on. I'm going to be seen with you. Are we dating in these scenarios? And I've never been great at managing my social media. The company did that, mostly."

His mouth fell open. "What?"

"The company—"

He waved his hand, and I shut up. "I heard you. I just can't believe it. I mean...I believe it. I just don't. I'm COO in addition to a lot of other things. How the fuck is the company arranging your social media, and I didn't know about it?"

"Well, maybe because you're in Paris and that is happening in New York?"

I had to blame the wine. I really had no business

commenting on the workings of his company. He narrowed his gaze at me. "Most things are done remotely now. No one has to be in the same location to work anymore. We have offices all over the world. I get up in the middle of the night to talk to Hong Kong."

I held up my hands in imitation of the way he did it. "Yes, except they're all there. And you're here."

He took a long sip of his own wine. "I can't be in the building with him. I almost skipped your wedding."

"Thank you for coming. To the hotel. I don't know that you needed to see me run down the aisle but...thanks for saving me."

He cleared my plate, sticking it in the sink. "Stop saying thank you."

"I like to say thank you. It's important to acknowledge when people do something for you. It's okay to feel grateful. There's nothing wrong with telling someone that you feel what they did mattered." I needed him to understand. "I don't know what I would have done today without you, and that is why I'm going to be honest with you. I can pretend to be your girlfriend. I don't even think it would be that hard." I took another drink. "You're very good looking. Who wouldn't want to be your girlfriend?" Yep, I'd just said that. I'd clearly had too much of the kick-butt red wine, but I wasn't going to stop. I liked it. "But they'll never believe it. I promise you that. Plus, he doesn't care. He disowned me. I have to pay him back for the wedding-that-wasn't." I perked up. "I love that phrase."

He took my hand. "They'll believe it. And I didn't know you were this much of a lightweight. Come on. You need a nap. We'll talk more at dinner."

"I have to eat again?" The idea was preposterous. I never consumed food in the middle of the day and then again at night. Breakfast, dinner, fine. In small doses, but...

He picked me up. "You have to eat again. I'm catching on to this being an issue for you. But yes, while you live here, you're going to eat. Those are not words I ever expected to say in my whole life."

"So you want me to pretend to be your girlfriend?"

He took the steps two at a time. "Yes. When we're in public. And in the meantime, I'm going to help you sort out your life so no one can ever take advantage of your good nature again."

"My good nature? I don't think I have a good nature particularly. I'm..."

He shook his head. "So help me, Layla. I don't want to hear you say one more bad word about yourself, or I might have to put you over my lap and paddle your ass."

I widened my eyes, his words sinking into my buzzing head like I'd sunk into the bath earlier. He was holding me, but I wished I could squirm. He'd just threatened to spank me again, and...I liked it.

Zeke laid me down in the guest room bed. He looked around. "Why are your clothes still in your suitcase?"

"I'm not sure if I'm staying." I yawned. "Why am I so tired? It's the middle of the day."

"Well." He took my sneakers off my feet and laid them next to the bed. "You've only been here a few days. You're jet lagged."

I shook my head. "I don't feel jet lag, ever."

"Everyone feels jet lag." He sat down on the edge of the bed. This should have been an uncomfortable moment. We didn't know each other, and yet it wasn't. It must have been the wine. I'd never felt this at ease with anyone, ever. "You've been through a lot today on top of that. And it turned out you get drunk on the equivalent of one glass of wine. Probably because you don't eat."

The last two explanations were probable. But I didn't buy

the jet lag. I never felt it. "What will you give me? In exchange for pretending to be your girlfriend to piss off my dad so you can find his secret stash of money? You know, besides spanking me."

He smirked at me. "You liked that idea. I saw it."

"I might not like it when I'm in my right mind."

He shrugged. "I wouldn't do it unless you were."

This was the strangest conversation of my life. "Okay, so besides that."

"I can make it so no one can ever do this to you again. You'll be in control of your own destiny. People will never try to intimidate or punish you again." He leaned forward. "Unless you want them to. Think about it. We can decide at dinner. Here's lesson one, and it's a freebie. Say no if you want to. Always. A lot. Say it so many times, people are actually afraid you will. Say it just because you want to fuck with someone's day." He paused. "Tell me no. Kick me out. Tell me you're not going to do what I want."

Zeke stared at me a long moment, which was when I realized he really wanted me to answer that. "No?"

"That's too bad. Now, I'll have to kick you out." He pushed away from the bed, and I waited for the wink. It took him a second longer than I would have preferred it to. "Take a nap, Layla. I'll see you at dinner."

I sat up. "No," I practically shouted at the door, and he laughed as he closed it behind him.

Who was Zeke Scott, and why was he so confusing?

Much as I was now yawning, there was no way I was going to actually sleep.

"Layla."

A deep voice called to me, pushing through a haze of sleep where I didn't have to think about anything. No, I didn't want to wake up. I liked it where I was. I was comfortable.

"Layla." This time the voice was accompanied by a gentle stroke on my head. I couldn't ignore the sweetness since I couldn't remember the last time anyone had woken me up pleasantly. It was strange, and the oddness of it was enough to draw me out of the happy place where I'd been so contented to stay.

Zeke was back in the place where he'd sat by me earlier. "There she is. You sleep hard."

I groaned. "Truthfully, I hardly sleep at all." I sat up on my elbows. "Maybe it all hit me."

"I woke you because I wanted to show you something. I try to see it every night when I'm home. You'll like it."

I rubbed at my face. "Okay. Give me a second."

"Yep." Zeke shot me another look before he exited my room.

This was a strange situation. I'd dreamed of him for years. Some of my most early sexual awakenings revolved around fantasizing about him. Now, here I was with him, in his house, having conversations I didn't really understand. He wanted me to make my father pay. That much I understood, and he was going to help me if I agreed.

I quickly washed my face and brushed my teeth. He was right. I'd slept hard. It was difficult to clear my head. I couldn't even remember if I dreamed. There was a headache forming behind my eyes the way that always happened when I actually did sleep after too long of not sleeping. I'd be back on track if I could actually rest steadily for the next few nights.

That was unlikely, considering things.

It seemed to make sense to just stay in my socks. I padded out to find him, which turned out not to be challenging. Two doors were open to the left of my room that led out to a balcony I hadn't seen earlier, because it was on the opposite side of the house from where I'd entered it.

He stood in the center of the balcony, starting at the changing sky.

It was sunset. I walked over and stood next to him, staring out at the city ahead of us as everything seemed to turn pink around us.

"It's beautiful."

He nodded. "I live here because there is nowhere else I'd rather watch sunsets in the world. I've been practically everywhere. And it never looks better than right here."

In the distance, the Eiffel Tower almost seemed to glow. "Is it true that Parisians didn't like the Eiffel Tower when it was first built?"

"I think that is mostly not true, but the story persists."

That was true of most things. The stories liked to persist, even when there wasn't an ounce of truth to them. "The radio tower one."

He nodded. "That's right."

I stayed quiet to watch the pink turn into orange and move over us. He didn't want to watch the sunset anywhere but here. That was sort of beautiful. I'd never spent much time watching them, even in places like this that were considered the most beautiful in the world. I had no new messages on my phone but stared at the time. It was nine-thirty. Sunset came later here. At least this time of the year.

Had it only been that morning I'd run from my life? "I may have made a huge mistake today."

"Maybe. Only time will tell, and if you take control of things, you can make it so it's just the opposite of that. Your greatest triumph. Your sisters are dependent on your father for their existence. You don't have to be, not anymore."

I supposed that was one way of looking at it. "They help him run the company now. Sure, it was nepotism, but they're bright and he knows how capable they are. Who can you rely on if not your family?"

"You couldn't rely on them. Not one of them." He turned from the view of the sunset to view me. "What do you think, Layla? Pretend to be my girlfriend, and I'll put you on a new path. No one even has to know it's fake if you don't ever want them to."

I winced. "I really hate lying."

"Except to yourself, apparently."

Okay, I'd had enough. I pointed my finger at him. "Watch it. You know I know how to smack you."

His smile was slow. "Yes, you do."

"So, watch it. You don't have to like me, but I'm not taking shit from you. Other people, okay, they've earned the right, but you are going to watch your mouth. You can think it, don't say it."

Zeke lifted an eyebrow. "Look at that, she has a backbone."

"Last warning. Next snarky remark, and I'm going to slap you."

He needed an answer. I was either agreeing to this with a man who could alternate between taking care of me and telling me I was pathetic. Or I was getting on an airplane and leaving Paris, putting this behind me, as I begged my father for another chance. The thought put a bad taste in my mouth. Sour, disgusting. I almost considered spitting over the side of his balcony, but to do so would go against everything I knew about behavior.

"I'll do it."

He nodded once, not looking at me as he turned back

toward the ever-disappearing sunset. "Good. Tell me what your situation is. Leave nothing out. If you owe money to drug dealers or the mob or a tribal leader in the middle of the Sudan, tell me all of it. Think of me as your personal confessor. I need the whole picture to figure out what to do."

I patted my hands on the balcony. It was hard to talk about myself. Oh, I could interview with the best of them. Platitudes and saying nothing of import. But this? It was different. "How do I know you can do what you say you can do? If you were so good at this, why would you need me?"

"Restraint."

That made no sense. "What?"

"When you're as rich as your father and I am, you know people who do all kinds of things. Whether you wanted to or not. At some point, you have to hire a security company who knows another company... Anyway, the reason I am trying to use you to get your father to dig his own grave is because I chose several years ago not to use the power I have to end his life."

A shiver moved through me. Was this for real? "You thought about killing my father?"

"Yes, and I have it on good authority that he has considered doing the same to me. More than once. Both of us are exercising a great deal of restraint. He ignores my messages and pretends I don't exist unless he absolutely must speak to me, and I do the same for him. We're at a stalemate not killing each other. Restraint."

I wanted to puke, and not from the delicious food I'd had earlier. "That can't be real. No. Business people don't..."

He shook his head, effectively silencing me. "Business is the number one reason for that kind of thing. Well, business and passion. People kill for that, too. Drug dealers and cartels...they're all in business."

My heart rate kicked up. It felt like I'd run a marathon. "Is that the kind of thing you and my father do?"

"No, princess." He looked away from me. "We are not in drugs or guns. Or anything like that. Just good old-fashioned runs-the-world business. And we're restraining ourselves from ending the other one, permanently."

If he wanted me to believe he could help me, he'd done that. If he really knew the kind of people who could do all that, then he probably could. I hated every second of it, and I wanted out of this life I hadn't known I was living on the outskirts of, immediately if not sooner.

But I had problems that had to be solved. And if dealing with gorgeous, and now scary, Zeke Scott could do that for me, then so be it. I'd use him as he used me at the same time, and we'd both walk away with what we wanted.

"I don't want my sisters hurt." I'd said that before, and I was sure I would again. In a world where I cared about nothing and no one cared about me, they were the exception. Maybe they weren't perfect, but they were mine.

He nodded. "I'm not taking your father's fortune, Layla. When I'm done, I'll just have what's mine. He'll have his half, and he and your sainted sisters are welcome to create whatever business they want with it."

"Don't call them that." I didn't like it, and I wasn't going to put up with him disparaging them.

"Layla." The sun was setting on him and this conversation. He wanted my answers, and I had to give them to him.

"I have no idea how much money is mine. I don't know anything. He's closed my credit cards, or he said he would. And emptied my account of his money. And I owe him for the cost of the mess I caused today." The sun sank into the horizon. "I'm dead to him. He's done with me."

Zeke stroked a finger down the edge of my cheek, and I shivered but not from cold. Was it possible heat could do that? Make you shiver with want? "He's not done with you. He hasn't even begun to know how not done with you he is. I'm going to let you in on a little secret."

I swallowed. "What's that?"

"He didn't mean that when he said it. Angry men make stupid mistakes. I'm counting on your father's temper to explode. There is nothing he'll hate more in the universe than the sight of you with me. So that is just what we're going to give him."

CHAPTER SEVEN

Z eke did like to eat really fine food. I was halfway through a steak I knew I wasn't going to be able to finish, a glass of red wine that he'd informed me when he poured was going to be it for me on the alcohol front, and the *pomme frites*, as he called them before he switched back to saying French fries and leaving it at that. I knew the word *pomme frites*. They were on some menus in English like that. Plus, he overexaggerated how he said it, which actually I found helpful instead of obnoxious because I at least knew I hadn't misheard.

It was awful always having to say 'what' only to realize you hadn't not heard, you'd just not understood.

I set down my fork, and this time, he didn't try to feed me more. We sat at his dining room table, fortunately, next to one another instead of across the table, which would have made me feel like we were playing at royalty in his pretend Versailles.

Zeke was so infallible in many ways, the fact that he'd hired a bad decorator gave me the smallest amount of pleasure. No one was perfect. Not even someone who looked like he did and had been as successful in life as he had been.

"Okay. Talk to me now." He sat back in his seat and sipped his wine, obviously not cutting himself off as he had done to me. I didn't mind. I was a lightweight, and we had to figure out how to have a conversation that didn't end with him having to carry me somewhere.

I tilted my head. This was late for eating. When we lived in Europe, my father had kept us on American eating times. He didn't like to eat past eight o'clock at the very latest. A ten o'clock dinner? It seemed almost obscene.

I was twenty-two years old. I could eat whenever the hell I wanted to, damnit.

"About what?" I'd told him all of my issues. I didn't think I had any more. As far as I knew, all of my debt was familial, and no one was going to come looking to collect with a gun pointed. Of course, now knowing what I knew, I supposed that was possible.

"About what you want to do with your life."

And there was the ten-million-dollar question. "I don't know." Same answer I'd been giving since they started to ask that in grade school. No idea. None.

"You're an influencer, right?"

I almost spit out my drink. "Look at you, knowing that word."

"I'm not that old, Layla. I know what an influencer is. You put on makeup and tell people what to buy. It's like a new take on old marketing. And that's what you do."

I hated to tell him the truth. "I don't actually post on my own Instagram account. That was—"

He held up his hand in that way I'd already discovered he did when he wanted me to stop speaking. "The company. Motherfucker." He crossed his hands in front of him. "Well, we can take that back from them, and you can stop being a walking advertisement for whatever they think you should be. Pick your own products. That'll be an income revenue for you, since you've already got that set up."

Zeke was going to want to kill me in a matter of minutes. "I don't want to be an influencer. I never did. It was just sort of something that got set up because of the book. And it kept going because it was good for public image to see me places."

He leaned forward. "What do you mean you don't want to do it? You're already doing it."

"I never wanted to."

"Then why..." He held up his hand, but I hadn't said anything. It was like he was stopping himself from speaking. "Okay. Not that." I waited for the yelling. This was when my father would probably start doing that. Zeke wasn't my father, thank goodness, considering the direction my thoughts often took with him, but he seemed like he might be the hollering type. Only he didn't. "You wrote a book."

He already knew I'd collaborated on it. "Yes."

"Did you like that?"

One of the staff I hadn't seen before came in, took our plates, and exited again quickly. "Why do they tiptoe around like they don't want to be seen?"

Zeke took a long sip of his wine. "I don't like people around. I'm easy to work with, in the sense that I leave people alone to do the things I hire them to do. But I don't want anyone under foot while I'm at home. It's totally a ridiculous problem to have. So when I hire them, they understand that they'll get paid very well with a lot of autonomy to make me feel like I'm alone at my house, even though there's a full staff here."

That was interesting. I sat forward. "How do you even have that conversation?"

"I don't. My manager does. Enough on this. You didn't

answer my question. Did you like writing the book? It's about fashion. You tell people what to wear."

No, he didn't understand, but I'd not expected him to. "I would never tell someone what to wear."

"Then what is the point of the book?"

Well, now that was a loaded question. But what was the point of anything when it came down to it? Why did we read anything? Do anything? "I tell people how to feel great in the clothes they already own, in their own style, and to make them feel really incredible in their own skin."

He opened and closed his mouth. "Why would you do that? Why make people feel good in their own stuff?"

I stared at him a long moment. Did I dare say what I wanted in response to his question? "Listen, maybe you've spent your whole life feeling incredible. I mean...look at you. You were probably always gorgeous. Even as a kid. Then you grew into how you are now. You wear the best cut suits and you wear them...they don't wear you. In jeans, you look like they created denim just so you could put them on your body."

"Layla, you're going to make me blush."

Hardly. He wasn't the type. I could tell. I was a redhead. We blushed better than anyone. Or worse, depending on your feelings on the subject. I ignored the jab. We both knew he wouldn't blush. "But most people go around feeling barely adequate in things they spend hours trying to decide if they want to buy. They stand there, and they can't decide what they hate themselves less in. I work on that with them. In the book."

"Because you feel so wonderful all the time." His eyes were practically daggers to my soul.

He couldn't have been more wrong if he tried. However, I wasn't going to enlighten him. Why should I? Zeke could see me as he wished, the way everyone saw me, even those who claimed to love me. They'd never see how I saw myself, how I felt inside.

I hated getting dressed, despised my clothes. The mirror was constantly my enemy, and there was never a time I had any clothes that I actually felt like wearing.

All of that being true, I answered him just the way he'd want me to, just the way everyone did. "Sure, I love getting dressed. It's so much fun."

"I see."

But he didn't. And he never would, which was utterly disappointing. But men were only ever tuned to your soul in fantasy. In real life, they didn't know how to touch you, didn't cater to your wildest desires, and certainly didn't know what it was that you didn't say aloud. Marriages were business arrangements, and I'd just been slow to figure it out.

"So, yes, I wrote a book and people liked it. But I think I said everything there was to say about that subject, and I'm not sure that there is anything left to write."

He rose. "There's always more to say. Textbooks are updated and celebrities seem to publish three or four autobiographies in a lifetime. We'll find you another ghost writer and go again."

If only it had been that easy. "Okay."

"I'm going to go into your bank accounts tonight and figure some things out for you. Can you be up by nine and ready to go get some coffee and breakfast?"

Nine? That was easy. I never slept very much. I was up way before nine most days. I chewed on my lip. "You can't get into my bank accounts without my information, passwords, whatever."

"My guy can get in. Frankly, it's shocking he hasn't been able to get your dad's yet. With your permission, I'll just have him do that. Unless you want to write them all down."

The sad thing? I wasn't certain I knew what they were. I

just kind of signed on through my computer which had all my stuff stored, but I didn't remember what the passcode actually was or even know how much money I had.

What had he called me this morning? Pathetic. Yes, that fit.

I shouldn't have slapped him. He'd just seen me more clearly than I'd seen myself.

"Layla? Is that fine?"

I smiled. The one I gave reporters who wanted my fall picks for fashion and I wanted to gauge out their eyes, because most people would never get to wear the fall picks either because of money or because they couldn't fit in the sizes that kept getting smaller and smaller. Hence, my need to run.

"It's fine. Thank you for your help."

He took his napkin off his lap. "You look like I just asked you if you wanted to go have a filling drilled in your mouth. What's wrong?"

"Nothing, I'm sorry. Long day. I appreciate the help." When in doubt, be polite. One of the nannies had taught me that.

Zeke shook his head. "You're lying, but that's fine. Keep your secrets. I don't want them if they don't apply to our arrangement. I think tomorrow night we'll start to be seen, to be photographed together. We'll go to a club that's opening. I'm over that scene, but I sometimes have to take clients to them. They like to be wined and dined. So we'll go tomorrow night."

I'd been to enough clubs in my life that I could actually choke on them. They were all the same when it came down to it, just the themes changed. "Sure. I brought clothes for Bali, not Paris at night. I am going to have to go shopping tomorrow."

"You look nice in that blue dress."

I looked down, sort of forgetting for a second what I'd put on. "Thanks. But this is not what the women wear to the clubs."

"You're right, of course." He smiled. "Shows you how much I think about women's clothing. I've always been more interested in getting women out of their clothing."

My cheeks heated up. He was blatantly sexual in a way I just wasn't accustomed to. Kit certainly hadn't been that way, even when he'd been quote-unquote in love with me. Zeke had invited me into his room with his shirt still off. He'd touched me as it suited him to do so. Carried me around. Threatened to spank me for talking badly about myself. And now he was talking about undressing women.

I was strangely naïve, considering the public opinion about me and my relationship status had kept me from being pursued in any blatant ways for a long time.

"I'm sure you are." I looked down at the table where my plate would have been had it still been there. I wished it were. I could pretend to eat more.

He took a long look at me that I could feel on my skin, even though I was staring down at the table. "You really are young, aren't you? For moments, I almost forget. And then it rushes back."

I was pretty sure he'd just insulted me again. That was Zeke's way with me so far. Be nice, helpful, flirty, and then mean. Wash. Rinse. Repeat. Amazing what I'd learned in less than twenty-four hours in his presence, and it hadn't done anything to lessen how much I wanted him. If only it was me who he was trying to get undressed.

Of course, he'd have to do all the work because I'd probably miss the cues, considering that I hadn't a clue how to flirt successfully.

"I don't think it's a crime to be twenty-two," I said finally, because something needed to be spoken or it was just going to get even more weird. "And I think I am young in a lot of ways and not young in others. In some capacities, I was born old."

"Fair enough." He actually ran his finger over the top of my hand, and I shivered from the contact. Why did he do that, and then in the next breath, be so obviously scorning of me? He was a confusing man. "Are you hoping to move the book writing into a fashion career? Making your own hand-bags? Or shoes? Or something?"

That was a fair enough question. "No. I'm not."

His eyebrows shot up. Maybe at how fast I'd said the no. "That might seem a logical next step. Take the success of the book—I looked, it was successful—and turn that into a career in fashion."

It might. But I didn't want to do that. "I know I'm frus-trating. Why can't or won't I just do what made sense? Take steps, make things happen. I was born into privilege. Use it."

"I'm not interested or concerned with your privilege. That was a non-answer you just gave me. Is it that you can't draw? Another I'm stupid thing? Because I'm sure in this day and age there is software..."

I held up my hand, imitating him, and he smirked at me as he stopped talking. "I can draw. It's not that. I just don't want to."

I was actually a great artist, when I used to do such things. But I hadn't given that a go since I was a child and wouldn't again.

"Wasn't your mother an artist? She was, right? I remember it was a big deal when she killed herself because out of the two of them, your mother and your father, she was the success at that point. Married the poor guy who was trying to make it. Had four kids and died. Her paintings go for a fortune."

My body went cold, the same way it did whenever she was

brought up, which was almost never. People knew better than to talk about her, because my father had made it clear that she was never to be brought up. Ever.

Your mother died eight years ago, Layla. I'm not going to discuss her now. Let dead be dead.

"My mother didn't kill herself." I was done with this conversation. It'd only been several hours, but I'd go back to bed rather than speak about this at any length. It hurt my stomach to think about her, made me want to pound things and declare that I wasn't that flighty, that somehow, I'd manage my life better. Even with all evidence to the contrary.

"I thought she did."

He had to know that I didn't want to talk about this. The man read my body language well enough to know when I was lying. He was pushing this subject, and since he was so big on the word 'no' I was going to use a version of it to end this night.

"She accidently took too many pills. She didn't kill herself on purpose. No one has any reason to think otherwise, and I'm going to bed."

"You haven't had dessert yet." As though he'd summoned him, the man who took our plates arrived with two more, setting them down in front of us. "And I apologize. That wasn't well done by me. I assumed you could talk about it, considering it happened twenty-one years ago. I get it. Some things aren't ever discussed. I have my own secrets, keep yours."

It wasn't a secret. He was just trying to get me to admit something I couldn't do because it wasn't true. She'd accidently overdosed on sleeping pills because she was so exhausted taking care of four children under four with an absent husband that she hadn't paid attention to what she was doing. It hadn't been suicide.

That was what I'd been told, and that was what I was going to believe.

Because I wasn't sure how I could digest the idea that she'd left us in our cribs to scream for twenty-four hours, until my father returned from his business trip to find us starving, soiled, terrified, and dirty. My brother wandered the house. Two years old. He'd tried to bring us bottles, but they hadn't had milk in them. Did anyone know if he'd seen her? Did anyone ever ask? Was it just me who didn't know?

I didn't remember any of that. Just what I'd heard over the years. My grandmother's whisperings. My aunt's drunken ramblings. The way that my mother's best friend, Lois, had stared at us with empty eyes one afternoon when she'd just had to see us again after a decade of not. That was when those things came out.

It was an accident. It couldn't be suicide. Because it was too awful to contemplate if it was.

We'd left Chicago after that and never lived there again.

The winters were hard there, or so I had heard.

"It's good. The chocolate mousse. Better than any I've ever had in restaurants."

He'd distracted my thoughts, and I stared down at the light brown concoction in the dish in front of me. "I haven't eaten dessert since I was twelve."

My words actually jarred him to the point that he always dropped his spoon. "What? Why? Layla, you are missing out on some of the great things in life. You know the expression, 'life is uncertain, eat dessert first'?"

"Because the standards of beauty are unfair. Because the nanny said I was getting fat in the hips. Because I didn't curve like Hope and Bridget did, not in the same ways. Because it was clear that they would use their brains in the future, and if I didn't want to end up in prostitution, I'd better figure out how to keep myself physically attractive so I could use it in other ways." I picked up the spoon and shoveled some of the sweet into my mouth. For a second, it was delicious. Rich. Frothy. Creamy. I took another bite and then another spoonful. Then it was too much.

I set the spoon down. It was...a lot to digest. I wasn't used to it, and the sweet was almost bitter because it was so much.

"Here." He handed me a glass of water he'd poured for me, but I hadn't drunk from yet. "Go easy, princess. You don't have to win a race. I won't pull it away from you if you eat it slowly, and I don't even know what not having dessert in a decade and then eating that would do to you. I bet you have to build up a tolerance."

I sipped the water and it did help to dull the sweet. "Thanks."

"My mother killed herself."

I dropped the glass, and the water rushed all over the table. In a second, I was up, grabbing my napkin to dab at it. "What? I'm sorry. Shit. Is it going to ruin the wood?"

Zeke grabbed my wrist. "It's water, Layla. Not lighter fluid. It'll be okay."

Two of his staff rushed from the kitchen, somehow alerted to what was happening, and wiped up the mess quickly. I sank back into my chair, staring at him.

"Note to self, don't startle Layla when she is drinking water."

I threw my napkin at him, and he grinned wider. "You told me just as I was drinking it, and I'm all jittery from that delicious mess."

"Mousse, not mess."

Now he was kidding? He dropped a bombshell like that and then made jokes? "I'm sorry about your mom."

"Yeah...it sucked." That might have been the most inarticulate I'd ever heard him. Sucked? Yes, I bet it did. In a massively terrible way. And maybe his own nonchalance about it was why he thought he could just ask me the way he had? Really push at it? Did he think we had that in common?

Did he want us to?

I knew very little about him. There were the press releases and the bio on the website. I'd looked at both of them at one time or another. He was from Michigan. He'd gone to a prestigious business school and competed in three different Iron Man competitions. That was all I really knew about his background.

Mother committed suicide... I could add that to his background now, only because he'd chosen to share it. That wasn't public knowledge, and considering the fact that my brother and sisters and I had to share a ton of ourselves for the sake of the company, it seemed a little off he hadn't had to do the same.

Except that Zeke had always been the man behind the man. My father made the money, and lost it so it seemed, and that put him out front. The genius. Zeke was the one who told him he was that. He sold the product, my father, to the world.

And didn't have to share himself in the process.

Only he just had. With me.

"How did she do it?"

He took his fingers, and in the shape of the gun, held it to his temple. "Quickly."

I winced. The imagery was enough. I didn't need to think about that. "Do they... I mean, not that there has to be a reason per se. But do you know why?"

"She owed a lot of money to a man who was going to do terrible things to her. Seemed like a good idea, I guess, to get out of the way."

That left him behind, and even if my mother hadn't been purposeful in her exit from this world, I knew what it was like to be the one left there afterwards. "How old were you?"

"I was eight. And I didn't have siblings. It was just her and me. I think she thought that my neighbor who we were close with would take me in. She didn't."

I'd had my father. He was absent and sometimes mean, but we'd wanted for nothing. "What happened to you?"

"What happens to kids in the United States who have no one? Foster care until I aged out at eighteen. Feels like it was a million years ago, not just two decades." He finished his wine. "Don't feel sorry for me, Layla. I decided the day they picked me up to take me into the system that I'd never need anyone to take care of me again. It's a great feeling. From the moment I became an adult, I've controlled my own destiny. That's what you can do, too. You'll see what I mean. I promise."

I leaned forward. "Why did you tell me?"

He held my gaze so long that my cheeks heated, but I refused to look away. Not until he answered me. "I don't know."

"I'll never tell a soul." I meant that to the depths of my own.

"I know, and I don't know how I know that either."

Well, at least I wasn't alone in my confusion.

CHAPTER EIGHT

"Hey, Layla," Zeke called to me on my way up the stairs to go to bed. I kept trudging upwards. I shouldn't have been tired again, but I was. Had I ever felt this old before? Ancient, really.

Finally, I got to my room, and I turned from the door to regard him from where he watched me from the top step. Despite my being tired, I knew I wouldn't sleep. Too much had happened in one day, I had too much to digest in my brain. Not to mention, I really wasn't used to that much food. My body might outright reject it.

"Yes?"

"You have security, usually, correct?"

I nodded. "Yes, but my dad took it away."

"My feeling is that we are probably paying for that through the company, so he can take it away, and I can give it back. Why did you have it? Stalkers?"

I shook my head. "It was never about me. Dad has people after him. He assumed that they might come after us to get to him. But I guess now that he's done with me, he figures he won't pay my ransom anyway. So why bother trying to keep that from happening?"

Zeke narrowed his gaze for a second, but I couldn't read his thoughts. I wasn't sure what he was considering. "I'll speak to Michael Li, and I'll see if he thinks you need security. He isn't going to let you get hurt because your father is being an ass. If you need a detail, you'll have one."

"I've never had a detail. I had one person who used to follow me around. It changed all the time. Michael stays with my dad, but he sends others out with us."

Zeke nodded. "Let me know if you need anything tonight. Otherwise, sleep well. We start at nine."

"Right."

Tomorrow, I would go to work—be his girlfriend until it made my father crazy enough that he gave up all his secrets to the people Zeke had trying to get that information.

In the meantime, I managed to put away all my clothes, since it looked like I'd be staying for a while. My clothes that would work for a beach vacation I would not be taking. I smiled. I could go romping around in my bikini if I really wanted to make a splash. For a half a second, I considered looking online to see what kind of write up I was getting after today, but I left it alone. There would be time for that pain and angst tomorrow. Better to not scroll before bedtime.

I washed, scrubbed, and moisturized my face before I dressed in a nightie I'd bought because I thought it might be sexy on my honeymoon. I remembered shopping for it online and thinking it looked like something a person should wear for such an occasion, not that I had wanted it. Always with the should.

Grabbing my phone before I plugged it in next to the bed, I shot off a message to Hope and Bridget. We used to have a group text going all the time, but lately, it had been silent. Were they talking to each other and just not me?

I wasn't going there tonight.

Hope you got home okay. Did I make a terrible mistake?

I shot off the note and then silenced it. I'd read their responses in the morning. I didn't suppose it mattered. It wasn't like I could hit rewind and undo anything. Potential terrible decisions didn't work like that.

The bed was comfortable. Someone had come in and made it while I'd been eating. Zeke's silent staff. It was weird that he was just down the hall and even stranger that I didn't find it odder than I did. He was a big presence. Always thinking, always circling back around, looking at angles. Then all of a sudden, he'd be funny or quirky. Followed by a mean remark.

Oh, and he was physically beautiful.

Alone in my room, I let myself dwell on that. The first time I'd been aware of him in the way that women noticed men was when I was thirteen. He'd been with my dad on the boat we were spending a week on for vacation. We'd hardly seen my dad. The nanny must have suggested the trip. She liked to fish and was trying to teach us how. Bridget had taken to it in the way that she did everything. Hope wandered off to read on the deck under shade, Justin was sleeping all the time, and I had spent the night getting sick because it turned out I suffered from sea sickness when on a boat. Having never been on one before, I'd had no idea, and it seemed no one particularly cared that it was happening to me.

They'd thought it would go away eventually, and fortunately it had, one day before we had left the boat.

Dad worked the whole trip. The yacht's Wi-Fi was being sketchy, so he kept going and coming from the boat. One of those times, he'd come back with Zeke. I tried to picture him how he'd looked that day. I'd made my way upstairs, hoping the sunshine might settle my stomach. It hadn't. They'd been seated on the deck together, drinking what I think had to be whisky. And they'd been laughing.

Things must have been very different between them then. Neither of them had looked at me as I'd sat miserably on the lawn chair watching them. I couldn't stop staring. Zeke had been...magnificent, just in the way he existed. In the way he sat. Took up space. Sipped the adult beverage I had been too young to consume.

I'd felt young, stupid, and ugly in my pink bikini that somehow hid more than it showed, and I hadn't wanted him to look at me in it. The words the previous nanny had slung at me about my weight the year before still resonated in my head—a weapon I would now wield at myself.

But then I hadn't cared about that, because something happened to me as I stared at him. I was suddenly uncomfortable in a way that had nothing to do with how self-conscious I was. No, my breasts were heavy, and there was a throbbing that started between my legs.

I hadn't known what was happening, but the longer I stared, particularly at his hands and the way his back muscles moved, the worse it had gotten. I'd run from the deck, sliding on some water that accumulated near the stairs and nearly killed myself slipping down them before I caught myself on the last one. By the time I'd made it to the bedroom I shared with my sisters on the yacht, I was out of breath and my heart raced.

No one had noticed my near death or maiming experience. Why would they? I was invisible. But oh, so alive in that moment. With my back pressing to the door to stop anyone getting in because there was no lock, I'd touched myself. The trouble had been I had no idea really how to do that. I still wasn't that great at it. I'd rubbed myself until it hurt and not achieved completion.

Orgasms were a constant problem for me. They didn't come easily or often, most of the time a frustrating endeavor that left me annoyed and feeling inept at something others were able to get in a matter of minutes, if they were to be believed. When I was finally over trying to relieve the need that wouldn't be fulfilled, I'd stepped back outside into the main sitting room just as the nanny had come down the stairs.

What was her name? I'd known it then, but not now. Couldn't remember. Not for the life of me.

"Hope, where have you been? I've been calling you."

She couldn't tell us apart. It really was a joke. She'd been with us a month and didn't have a clue which one of us was which. We didn't even try to look alike. How did she not know? I ignored her. If she wanted me to speak to her, she had to get my name right. It wasn't my problem she wanted Hope. If she'd wanted me, I'd have answered her.

"Answer me." She stomped her foot. I wished she were the first nanny to stomp her foot at me. It happened often. We must have been frustrating as hell to deal with. I mean how many adults stomped their feet?

"Well, she might, if she were Hope." Zeke leaned on the side of the stairs before he walked toward the bathroom. "But I don't think Layla is responsible for answering for Hope." He rolled his eyes and headed on his way.

The nanny breathed heavy, her cheeks red and her gaze angry, not at Zeke but at me. As though that whole thing had been my fault. I didn't care. Let her be furious and embarrassed. He'd known which one of us I was.

That had been huge.

In the current time, I rolled onto my stomach. What did I know now? That kind of physical reaction to someone would be very unusual for me. I didn't throb easily, and I mostly shied away from too much physical contact. It was hard enough to protect myself emotionally without someone touching me in my most private of parts.

But Zeke could still do it for me. He had great hands I wouldn't mind on my body. And I'd never get over the fact that he had hardly ever seen me in his whole life, and yet he'd known I was Layla and not Hope.

Beautiful, infuriating man.

I fell asleep thinking about that.

With the sun coming through the shades, I woke up fast. Disorientation hit me, and for a long second, I had no idea where I was. But then the day before rushed at me like a movie playing in my head. I'd run from my wedding, and I was staying at Zeke Scott's house. I sat up, putting my face in my hands.

It was eight-thirty in the morning. I almost couldn't believe my eyes. I never slept this late. Ever. And I was due to be ready to leave with Zeke in half an hour. First day on the job, I couldn't be keeping him waiting.

I checked my phone. My sisters had both answered me. They'd gotten home, they were fine, and no I hadn't made a mistake. Bridget had gone so far as to tell me that Kit was a stupid asshole and she was glad to never have to see him again. I smiled at that. When Bridget got mean, she really got mean.

I stepped down on the floor and groaned. Yep, my feet still hurt. That was the trouble with foot injuries. They lasted, and I couldn't forget about them. I limped into the bathroom and abruptly stopped. Next to the sink were bandages and pads as well as antibacterial lotion and an ace bandage. That had absolutely not been there when I'd gone to bed. Had it?

I really didn't think so.

I stared down at it for a second. Had I slept through someone bringing it in here? I wasn't a heavy sleeper, usually.

I woke up to any small noise in my apartment, and sleeping in the same bed with Kit had been next to impossible because he snored. But I had not heard anyone come in and leave these supplies here.

Had I been snoring when he came in? Did I snore? I shook my head. Well, if he'd come in when I was asleep, again, then there was nothing I could do about if I were sleeping loudly. It was actually really nice of him to think of this stuff, and I was absolutely going to need them. I washed my face, brushed my teeth, stuck my hair in a messy bun because I didn't have time to deal with it, and brushed my lips with a little bit of lip gloss. I was barely presentable, but it would have to do.

I had two pairs of yoga pants with me that I'd intended to use as my get up and eat breakfast attire at the resort in Bali. I shoved on the black pair and covered it with a long T-shirt I sometimes slept in. It was white and plain.

The final step was to doctor up my feet. They looked worse than yesterday. The bruises I'd gotten were changing colors as bruises were apt to do, and I'd destroyed my pedicure. When my feet healed up a bit, I'd go get that fixed. I bandaged where I could, padded where I needed it, and shoved my sneakers back on.

I got out into the hall just at the same moment Zeke came out of his rooms. He was dressed in a pair of jeans that were darker than the ones he'd been in yesterday and a black T-shirt. His boots were what caught my attention. They were tall, like he might wear on a motorcycle.

"Morning. Sleep okay?" He closed the door to his bedroom behind him and took a step toward me. The fresh scent of the shower was on him, and I breathed in deep through my nose, hoping he didn't notice but not able to stop myself from doing so.

"I did." I smiled. "Thanks for the stuff for my feet."

He nodded. "You're welcome. I didn't want to wake you. I knocked and waited, but you were out cold, so I just left it and didn't disturb you."

"I usually wake up. Guess I must have been exhausted. What time did you come?"

He motioned toward the stairs. "About midnight when I thought about it. I was closing a deal when it dawned on me that you might need more stuff for your feet. So I went out and grabbed the stuff for you and came back. Glad I didn't wake you."

Like everything else with this man, I should feel weirded out that he was in there while I slept, but I didn't. My reactions to Zeke weren't what I would have expected.

He stopped on the stairs. "I debated about whether to bring it in. You were sleeping, but I wanted you to have it in the morning. I was in and out. I didn't look at you or anything. Believe it or not, I do know what privacy is."

I laughed, his words surprising me. "Okay. How about next time you knock louder and wake me? But I don't mind that you did it, even if I should."

"I can't imagine I'll have another reason to come in your room while you're asleep."

That was actually disappointing. I could think of some reasons I might like him to come in. My memories from the night before felt fresh. He had been pivotal to my life, and he didn't even know it. I was never going to tell him. Some things like those kinds of memories were the kind you took to your deathbed and kept to yourself.

"We're going on my motorcycle. Unless you object. I prefer it this time of day."

"I've never ridden on one."

He tilted his head. "Well, this is a morning for firsts then."

I followed him to the garage, which was outside the guard house and impressive on the inside. He hadn't parked his

Porsche himself yesterday, so I hadn't seen that he had ten cars and three motorcycles before. I smiled. This was such a guy thing to do. Lots of money and lots of fun things to drive. But there I went gendering. There were women who would do this, too. I just wasn't one of them.

What did I spend money on? I supposed clothes, but that wasn't a choice. I didn't love clothes or even want that many around. It was more like a necessity. Truthfully, I had no idea. I didn't really spend on things.

That was funny. I'd never thought about that before.

"Come on." He handed me a helmet. "Let's go. Put your arms around my waist and hold on tight. When I lean in a direction, you lean that way, too."

That sounded easy enough.

I did just as he said, and soon we were on the road. Although there was some traffic, he seemed to know where to go to avoid it, and I could see why he loved this. I leaned against his back and held on, squeezing him if I got nervous. The wind was fantastic as it whipped at our bodies, and by the time he pulled into a space, my heart raced, and I wanted to keep going. Was it possible to just ride like that forever and ever?

We were near the hotel with the birds, but instead of going in, we entered a café. Everyone lifted their heads to greet him, speaking fast and loudly. They had smiles on their faces. Zeke took my helmet and set it next to his in the corner as he took what I bet was his regular table.

A waitress came over and greeted Zeke with warmth, kissing him on both cheeks. She briefly regarded me, but not for long, and then disappeared into the kitchen.

"This is really nice." It was a warm décor with about a dozen small tables that didn't seat more than four at a time. Mostly they were two headers. Two coffees appeared before us as well as the carafe where I guessed we could pour more into our own cups if we wanted. I appreciated the coffee. I wasn't big on eating breakfast. Well, I usually had something. But after all the eating we did yesterday, it would be fine to skip.

"It's a favorite. Everyone in Paris has a favorite café. This is mine. I eat here every day."

Someone across the place said something, and Zeke smiled before he shouted something back. "Why this one instead of any other?"

A basket was placed in front of us, and this time, the waitress stared at me longer. I made eye contact with her. Was she waiting for me to understand something that had been said? Because I really didn't have a clue.

She pointed at me, and Zeke nodded, this time answering her in English. "Yes, this is Layla. She doesn't speak French."

"Oh." The woman clapped her hands together. I took a long look at her. She was beautiful and sparkled in that way that French women did. Was it in the water? "Yes, I follow you. Yesterday you ah…"

I finished for her. "Ran around Paris in a wedding dress. Yes, that was me."

She laughed. "But now I understand. New York socialite. You are sleeping with Zeke. You leave your fiancé. It all makes sense."

Did it? I almost corrected her, but that was what we were saying. I was supposed to be dating Zeke, which would mean I had thrown over Kit for him. Wow. I'd really not thought that through. It was going to piss off the Allards to no end. There were all kinds of ramifications to this I hadn't considered. Yes, it might hurt Kit, but I doubted it. But Mrs. Allard? Oh, yes, she was going to be mad. Laura was going to have a fit.

And maybe any chance she'd give that exorbitant amount of money to my father would go away permanently. It might have already, but still…if she'd considered doing it despite my blunder, she wouldn't now.

In the light of day, with exhaustion not weighing on me, I could see this much more clearly. But there was no question that Ezekiel Scott understood it perfectly. I'd agreed to this. So in for a penny, in for a pound. Or euro, as the case happened to be.

I put out my hand across the table. If we were a couple, Zeke should take it. For his part, he didn't hesitate. The man I was about to create an elaborate lie with caressed my skin with his thumb. He had hard, callused fingers, like he used his hands and not like he regularly got manicures. I stared at his nails. They were clean but not polished.

"I'll be right back." The waitress turned and rushed off.

With his free hand, Zeke pointed to the basket. "Eat."

I hadn't realized that the basket was loaded with pastries. Wow. That was a lot of carbs. I stared at it. Zeke let go of my hand. "Going to make me feed you?"

No, not in public. I had to draw a line about how far I was willing to go in that direction. Instead of eating, I sipped my coffee. It was delicious, already creamed. I tended to drink mine black, but this was fine. Better than that. Outstandingly tasty.

"We have a lot of things to do today, Layla. We have to clothe you, and then you have to come out with me tonight. And we have to talk about your future. None of that is going to happen with an empty stomach. Would you rather have some eggs?"

I took out the croissant. "The eating thing can't be a constant issue between us. I don't eat very much. I'm not naturally…thin. But I need to stay that way. It works for you, too, okay? If I gain weight, they're going to say you got me pregnant. Do you want that? Or do you want me to be the person who people follow because I'm one of the redheads?"

"When your feet feel better, we can run together."

That was all he was going to say to my pronouncement? Really? I angrily buttered my croissant. It was possible to sort of abuse it so that I could take my frustration out on the food instead of him.

He ate, too, stopping only to watch a woman in the corner who started to talk loudly. I followed his direction. She wasn't crying, but she wasn't happy. I guessed her to be maybe forty years old, and across from her was a woman who resembled her a great deal, a younger version. Both dark haired. Both blue eyed. Strong, striking cheekbones.

They could be on the cover of something.

"Is she okay?" I asked him. I didn't have to understand to hear tone.

"She's not happy. She's supposed to be leaving her to go for a walk with a man she wants to date. First time since her divorce, and she's calling herself a bunch of names." He kept his voice down. "Renee has lots of money, very comfortable. But this is a first, and she's not feeling...confident."

I turned in my seat and looked at her quickly before she noticed and then back at Zeke. She was lovely. But I could see it in the way she was holding herself in the chair, the way her daughter wasn't making eye contact with her. It was already going to be a disastrous date, and it hadn't happened yet. Just based on how she was feeling right now.

"I can help."

He leaned forward. "How can you do that?"

"I...know I can."

This was sort of what I did. In a weird way that I'd never done before. But I wanted to. The poor lady. Why start out behind? If she wanted that date, she should have it go well from the start. There were enough things that could go wrong.

"Okay." He indicated toward her. "Her daughter knows

who you are. Said it when we walked in. And they speak English."

I rose. I was going to go bother a stranger in the hopes that I could make her day better. I must have been out of my mind, except I had to do this. I just had to.

CHAPTER NINE

There was no polite way to approach someone about what I was going to do. I mean, it was none of my fucking business. I had no reason whatsoever to get involved in this woman's day. She might tell me to get the hell away from her, probably in French so I wouldn't understand her, but I'd get the gist anyway, and I'd be humiliated in front of a café of strangers. And Zeke, who thought of me pretty badly anyway. He'd seen my bank account, and I didn't know what was in it yet, but I was sure it wasn't pretty.

But I felt compelled, the same way I had to run down the aisle away from Kit, and apparently, it was a week where I did what I wanted, damn the consequences.

"Hi," I said to them, and the daughter lit up like a lightbulb. She smiled at me and then at her mom. "I'm sorry to interrupt. This is none of my business. But I thought I could help."

The daughter said something in French, and I winced. Apparently, Zeke was not going to help me with this. Fine. "I'm sorry. I don't speak French." I made a face like I was an idiot as I tapped my temple. "I just never learned. Do you by any chance speak English?"

"Why yes, of course." Her accent was thick, but she was entirely understandable. "I'm surprised you are with Zeke if you don't."

"Mother." Her daughter's accent matched her own. "She's the redhead. Of course, he's with her. She's famous."

I shook my head. Time for the line. "Oh, I'm hardly the only redhead. There are still enough of us around, even if we're rare. Why, my sisters are both redheads, too." I never said it exactly the same. But I got the point across each time. "So, if you don't have a problem with me absolutely not minding my own business, I can help you."

"Oh." Her daughter got to her feet. "Layla, I am Danette, and this is Mother, Renee."

I smiled and nodded, trying to remember my manners in this mannerless situation that I'd created for myself. "I have a little experience with clothes."

Danette said something to her mother in French, and eventually, her mother rose. "I'm afraid it may be a helpless situation. I don't have time to go shopping."

This was where most people misunderstood what I liked to do. There was absolutely no need to go to a store. We just had to adjust how she wore what she was wearing so that she felt better in her own clothes.

"No need." I smiled. "We're not going shopping."

She'd put on a red skirt. It was long, hitting past her knees, and it showed off her thin stature that still managed to be curvy. Her daughter was just a little bit taller than she was. They were really beautiful. "Good genes in your family."

They both beamed at this. Renee had also matched the red skirt with a black turtleneck T-shirt. She'd tucked that in. I could see the problem immediately.

We'd gathered a crowd. Everyone but Zeke had crowded

around to see what I was doing. They spoke to each other like they were a crowd that all knew each other. Or at least that was how it seemed. Was this a regular stop for everyone in here?

"Is it okay if I touch you?"

Renee gave a little shrug. The kind a person gave when they had no idea if what the other person said to them was insane. I must truly seem that way.

I took it as a yes. I was already into this craziness, I needed to do a good job. But it would be easy with Renee. She just needed the slightest adjustment. I pulled her shirt out, letting it hang loose. The way the skirt hit her did nothing for her slim waist, it was more like a hip hugger. Very pretty, but probably just the reason she didn't feel quite right at the moment. But I understood what she was trying to do which was show off the waist to begin with, only that wasn't going to happen unless we adjusted her slightly.

I looked at her daughter. "Do you need that coat?"

"No." She smiled and took it off, handing it to me, which I quickly put on Renee. It was faux leather and lightweight. She'd probably be a little hot in it, but if the walk turned into lunch and Renee was feeling all kinds of more comfortable, she could take it off then. I stepped back to look at the whole presentation. Something was missing. It was always about the small details. Maybe it was just me, but I really felt like it was the small details that made all the difference with the outfit.

I spun around and looked at the women behind me. "Do you know each other?"

"Why, yes," the blonde, taller woman answered. "We are very close friends."

"On weekends, we are all here," Danette supplied.

The blonde, whose name I should learn and would in a minute, wore a beautiful piece of costume jewelry. I had a pretty good eye for telling what was real and what wasn't.

And sometimes I preferred the look of the so-called cheap stuff better. Hers was a long black chain with a gold medallion on the bottom. She'd matched that with a gold webbed bracelet.

"Can I borrow your jewelry?"

Her eyes widened. "You like them?"

"Yes, they're beautiful, but what's more, they'll look great on Renee. Is it okay?"

She quickly handed them to me, and I turned them over to Renee. "Go look at yourself."

The woman smiled at me, the biggest one she'd given me as of yet, and she hadn't even seen herself yet. It was as much the process of anything. I smiled at Danette. "Your mom is gorgeous."

She outright squealed, and I took a step back. "You're Layla, the redhead. Did you really leave your fiancé for Zeke like they're saying?"

"I did." The lie tasted bitter, but I'd agreed to this. "We're together."

"He is so handsome. I wished my mother might date him, but she said she isn't his type. And he only dates four days. Then it's all over. And we like this café too much."

Some of her English had gotten a little mixed up, but I understood her completely. Well, I didn't know how long Zeke and I would stay together. I supposed that was up to my father and how he behaved toward the whole thing.

I took Danette's hand. "Thanks for letting me fix up your mom. She's going to feel great now."

Sure enough, Renee emerged from the bathroom with a grin on her face. There was actual applause all around her for that grin, and soon, everyone had started speaking French again. I smiled at Renee and made my way back to my table.

He lifted his lids but didn't say anything else to me. If he had even a thought about the few minutes I'd been away from the table, he wasn't going to share them. I took a long sip of my coffee as people swarmed here and there before either sitting back down or leaving.

The gorgeous blonde who had loaned Renee her necklace came by. She stared at me for a long second before turning to Zeke and saying something to him in French. I expected him to tell her to speak English, but he didn't do that. Instead, he ended up narrowing his eyes and saying something short that sounded almost curt.

She finally spoke to me, speaking in a way I could understand. "You are young and charming. That was a very nice thing that you did for a very nice person who deserves it, and you couldn't even know that. The young people tell me you are famous for that sort of thing, for your beauty."

My cheeks were red. She was complimenting me but not at the same time. I didn't know who she was, but I'd be surprised if she weren't successful at something I should know about. She wanted me to be impressed with her, too. "You were the one with the beautiful jewelry and the generous spirit to help her. Thank you for doing that. It was really nice of you. I'm sorry, I don't know your name."

Her smile wasn't kind. "My name is Isobel. And Zeke and I are long-term friends."

The way she said that made sense now. It wasn't me she didn't like. It was that I was sitting with Zeke. They'd slept together, I didn't know who she was, she thought I should, and this was going to be a giant mess.

"I think you must be late now, right?" Zeke's tone dripped with annoyance. "And let me finish breakfast with my girlfriend."

"Girlfriend?" Isobel threw her hair over her shoulder. "Oh, how charming. Be careful, little redhead. He moves through us like he might tissue paper. See you all next weekend."

He sat back in his seat while Danette and Renee rushed

by to thank me on their way out the door. Such a whirlwind of things happening. Isobel was gone, and I was glad for it. I buttered my croissant and ignored the pain in my stomach while I did. I'd had half a dozen conversations with this man over the last twenty-four hours. I had no business whatsoever caring who Zeke did or didn't sleep with, or how many days he usually let that last.

The croissant tasted delicious. He was right. I needed energy. I'd focus on that. I chewed and swallowed. Once, then again.

"What you just did, that was a really nice thing." He crossed his arms over his chest. "Do you do that a lot? Tell people what they should wear?"

I sighed. "I didn't tell her what to wear. She picked out her clothes. I just fixed her in them. I'm not a stylist. I didn't purchase her clothing, I didn't dress her in them. I made her feel better in what she'd done."

"And people need that? To feel better in their own choices?"

"Sometimes." Maybe he never did, and so he'd never understand it.

"I don't know about women's clothing. You untucked her shirt, you accessorized her. It was like a transformation from one version of her on the inside to the next, like she lit up. She spends every Thursday night volunteering in shelters with the homeless. Her daughter is really kind. And they both got fucked over by a man who moved on and moved away." He sipped his own coffee. "Love and marriage. Who needs that kind of pain? In any case, you made her day. A complete stranger, so I'm more concerned with what that means about you. I haven't seen anyone do something like that...maybe ever."

He was making more of this than it had to be. "Like you

said, I untucked her shirt. I didn't find a way to cure the common cold. I'm done. I'm full. What are we doing now?"

"We're going to get you some clothes. You can't actually be done."

"Don't push it." I glared at him. "I don't want any more."

He twitched his mouth like he might smile but didn't. "Okay. We'll move on. Get you some clothes."

"Are the stores open on Sunday? And I can afford this?" He still hadn't told me what money I had.

"You need clothes while you're here to do what I need you to do, so I'm going to pay for that. Don't argue. It's not charity. And no, you don't have a lot of money in your account. You have no debt. He paid off your credit card before he took it away, which didn't have much on it anyway. You are remarkably thrifty, considering things. Either that, or Kit was paying for everything. In any case, that is done." He set down his coffee cup. "And something is fishy. That book was a hit. Look at this room. You should have a lot more money than you do. I think he stole from you when he emptied your account. I'll prove it. And in the meantime, open you a new account, get you set up with a new future he can't touch, and tell your father he can't fuck with your life anymore."

Sounded like a plan. I hoped he could do all of that fast because there was no way what I'd just done hadn't been photographed. Someone had held up their phone and snapped a picture. I could almost guarantee it. I could always feel when I had eyes and camera lenses trained on me. It was like ants crawled on the back of my neck. I'd learned to ignore it. Being stared at was part of my life.

But I'd felt it in the café. My father might very well know I was dating Zeke the second he opened his eyes back in the United States five hours from now. This could all be over very, very soon. And I was sure Zeke would keep his word and help me. Still, it was a tall order, all the things he promised, and in my experience, men didn't want much to do with me after they'd gotten what they wanted.

I might not be Zeke's pretend girlfriend very long. He might even beat his four-day record with me. Less than twenty-four hours before he put me on a plane back to New York.

Riding on his motorcycle was no less exciting the second time. We arrived at a boutique that didn't look open when we pulled up, but was remarkably available the second we arrived at the door. I shot Zeke a look. He'd clearly arranged this.

I steeled my spine and ignored whatever look he was sending me as he handed his credit card to the saleswoman and told her something in French. I knew how to do this. I'd bought a lot of clothing in my life, and it wasn't going to take long to figure out what I needed. All of it would be expensive, even the casual wear would be fancy in its own way, and I'd look exactly like I needed to by the time I walked out of this place.

Without waiting for her to say anything to me, I strode to the back. Better to just get this over with. I had a role to play, and I was going to do it. As fast as I possibly could.

Zeke looked up from his phone when I exited. "Everything okay?"

"Yes, I'm just done. All taken care of." I shrugged. "Are we going to bring all of it back on your motorcycle?"

"No." He rose. "They'll deliver it later today. That didn't take very long. I thought we'd be here quite a bit longer."

Maybe for someone else. It would be fun to be let loose in a clothing boutique with women fawning over them, everything they could dream of presented to them. For me, it was a regular ritual. I knew what I needed, how to get it, what would fit and what wouldn't. I didn't want anything I didn't need and none of it was fun.

"Guess I'm fast."

He put his hand on the side of my face, cupping my cheek. "You're not happy. Did they not have the things that you want? This place is always being talked about. I thought..."

I placed my own over his. It was a strange but also beautiful moment. No one touched me like this. There was an intimacy to the act that he hadn't earned, and yet I wouldn't have had him drop his hand for anything in the world. "I don't like clothes. They're a necessity. I have to look like I'm supposed to look. But it's not..."

I couldn't finish that sentence because I really didn't know how to explain it. Shopping did nothing for me. That wasn't what I wanted out of life.

The salespeople were staring at us. I could feel it. That icky, creepy-crawly feeling on the back of my neck. They'd been nice enough, but now they were vultures wanting to chew up this moment by just looking at it with their uninvited eyes.

"Try. Tell me what you mean."

I swallowed. "Why?"

"Because I want to know."

That was hardly a reason. I didn't owe him access to my soul, to my inner thoughts, or insecurities. I'd not promised him any of that. Yet, I wanted to tell him because he asked, because he was the first person to ever do so.

"We're not alone."

He dropped his hand at my words, and I let him go. "Okay, Layla. I'll take you at your word. You got what you needed. Come on. Let's go do something fun."

His phone dinged, and he grabbed it, looking down. "It's Michael Li getting back to me about your security.

Outside." I followed him until we both stood next to his motorcycle.

"I'm here with her now," Zeke told Michael. I was only hearing bits and pieces of their conversation over the noise on the street. "Yep. No. Do I need to be worried?"

I touched the seat on his motorcycle. He wanted to do something fun. I'd be up for riding in circles all day at high speeds, feeling the wind and letting him drive and drive, until we were both so tired, I couldn't see straight for it. That wasn't likely. He had to work tonight, entertain clients, and I had to go with him and wear the gold dress I'd picked out.

Zeke swung around. "No immediate threats that they're worried about. Just the constant problem of your father owing money to people he should never have gotten into bed with to begin with. But that's not new. He had to move you every two years because of that your whole life. If something changes, Li will send security on my request and your father can screw himself if he tries to stop that. Michael might have done it anyway and damned the consequences. I think he's likely to go one of these days anyway. Start his own firm."

That was interesting. I'd never thought of Michael as being part of the company. He was like a separate entity altogether, but I guessed he was. Like I was. Like Zeke was. It was that place that connected us, that brought us all together.

"I promised you fun."

I smiled at him. "Fun is such an arbitrary word. For example, you seem to find eating to be a lot of fun. I don't think of it that way."

"Ah, but you will." His smile was contagious, so I gave him one back. "We're in France. You can't help but fall in love with food here. Give it time. You'll be actually hungry when it's time for a meal one of these days."

I groaned. "You want me to fit in those clothes you just bought me, right?"

"I'll buy you new ones. I'd rather have you fed than fashionable."

That went contrary to what we were actually doing together, but I loved it so hard, I pretended he could actually give a shit right then. I was choosing the delusion, and even knowing it was that, I liked it. When Zeke was this way, it was easy to like him.

"So no more shopping. And I'm guessing you're not going to want a spa day either."

I didn't mind them when I needed them, but I'd had my fill getting ready for my wedding. "I think I'm all pampered out, and my poor feet... No pedicure yet."

"Got it. Then I have just the thing. Come on." He handed me the helmet. My hair, thanks to the bun I kept putting up and taking down, was actually holding up pretty well despite the abuse from the helmet.

"Where are we going?" I took it from him.

"You'll have to trust me." He tilted his head. "Can you do that?"

Could I? I didn't do so easily. "Why did you stay with my father so long when you knew he was doing things like getting into trouble with very bad men? Why didn't you get out earlier?"

He leaned forward. "I've trusted you with the secret about my mom. You haven't done that with me yet. Not really. What you're asking me, it goes to the heart of a lot of things about me that I keep entirely to myself. You want to know? You're going to have to earn it. I extended my hand, and you haven't taken it yet."

I swallowed. He meant what had happened in the store. The clothes and why I didn't want them, didn't like them, found the whole thing to be just...like going to the dentist. Trying on clothes was like pulling teeth for me. He wanted to know why.

"At some point, it became what I was known for. When I dropped out of college because, let's face it, I didn't belong there, fashion was decided as my thing. And at some point, it became all I was. But it's not all I am. I don't even like my clothes. I tell people to enjoy their style, to look their best as they are, and I've never, not one day in my life, looked like me. I don't even know what it is but it's not...shown up yet."

Zeke set down his helmet on top of the bike. "So what you're saying to me is that you think you're a fraud, and clothes shopping only highlights that for you."

He'd hit the nail on the head. "Yes."

"They really fucked you up, Layla Radford. But that's okay. All the best people I know are totally bent in the head."

I didn't see how that was a reasonable response to what I'd just said to him. I told him I basically felt like getting dressed was participating in some kind of fraudulent activity and that was his response?

"Zeke..."

He kissed me. I didn't see it coming, and I wasn't sure he'd planned it. One second, he stood next to me, and the next he drew me to him hard and kissed my lips gently, a stark contrast to the way he held me still. I closed my eyes, totally surprised by the caress as I gave myself over to it at the same time.

Zeke pressed his mouth deeper, and I wanted it to never stop. My body seemed to come alive. I didn't know what to do. I'd never been kissed like this before, so unplanned, so spontaneously, and my breasts hardened in the seconds that he held me.

He pulled back, smoothing his thumb over my mouth. "You're so young. I need to leave you alone."

If he'd dumped cold water over my head, he couldn't have destroyed that second any better. "I was going to be someone's wife. I'm not that young, I assure you."

"Even if you were waking up as Mrs. Kit Allard this morning, you'd still be young. Too young for me. I don't do love and romance. I do temporary. Heat. Sex. Fun. You're living with me until we get this sorted. I won't be another man who fucks up your life."

Now wasn't the time for an argument. I knew enough to know that I wanted Zeke to do those things with me, and I was going to have to convince him when his guard wasn't as up as he'd just placed it.

That kiss had shown me I wanted more. And maybe for now, the best thing I could do was to have no-consequence sex with the only man I'd ever wanted to have it with.

CHAPTER TEN

I got what I'd wished for, and for a while, Zeke drove me around Paris on his motorcycle. While we'd never lived in Paris, I had been here many times. Still, I'd never seen it from the back of a motorcycle, clinging to a man who had kissed me into plotting how I could have sex with him in the future. At no time did it feel like I had ants crawling on me or any other upsetting feeling.

We were two people wearing helmets, darting around traffic, and enjoying the heck out of the pleasant weather. No one knew us in those moments, and for just a little bit, I wondered if I was getting to know myself better. I was a woman who liked the wind to hit her body at high speeds, to depend on someone else for my safety, and to try something new on a Sunday that she'd never done before. These were all things I hadn't realized when I woke up that morning.

Eventually, we stopped, and I let my feet ache a little bit while we walked around Montmartre, admiring the work of the artists. Or at least I was. Zeke could go quiet for periods of time, and while I didn't find it unnerving, I did have to wonder what it was that would catch his attention and hold him so quiet. I'd shared with him, and he had yet to answer my earlier question.

I didn't want to ruin this time by asking again. I would, it was important I understood, both for myself and for the sheer curiosity because he knew things about my life I didn't know. My dad got into trouble, and that was why we'd had to leave? Why didn't I know that?

Why hadn't I asked?

I stopped to admire the work of one artist who did his in pencil and charcoal. It was a dramatic effect and different than the others I'd been looking at. When he spoke to me, I smiled. It was really the only thing I could do when this happened. I'd not been traveling that much lately, and I'd not asked myself why, but maybe it had to do with this problem. I hated not understanding.

"He wants to know if you want your portrait done. He says it would be a gift to his pencil to sketch you."

Zeke translated for him before answering the man. I wondered how many times he'd had to already tell people I just didn't get what they were saying to me. It wouldn't be such a big deal if I hadn't tried to learn, if I'd never made the attempt. Most people probably thought that. I hadn't studied French, fine. But I had tried. And Spanish. German. Chinese. All of them had been a sad failure, with the schools suggesting to my father he get me tested for one thing or another. He never did, and the Fs didn't matter because he'd paid to get me into school anyway, where I had promptly failed. Again.

Strangers didn't know all of this, but I did, and it was a constant bang in my head to try to deal with it. Better to just stay home.

"Well, I'll do it if you'll do it."

No way was Ezekiel Scott going to sit still and let the artist sketch him. There was no way. He smiled at me. "One thing you should know, while I'm not a jackass about it, I do find it difficult to resist a real challenge when it's presented to me. Like I'm not going to jump off the Eiffel Tower. That's stupid. But show you that I will absolutely get my portrait done? Sure. I'll do it. If you do it with me."

I turned to look at him straight on. "Okay."

He said something to the artist, and there we were, seated together, letting a stranger try to capture us in that moment.

"Hold on," Zeke said before he must have repeated it to the gentleman who was going to try to sketch us. He was older, with a beard and a kind smile.

Zeke moved us until I sat in his lap, with his chin on my shoulder. With the sun behind us and Paris looking as beautiful as I'd ever seen it, we stayed very still and let the man with all the talent attempt to capture us.

Eventually, he said something that made Zeke groan and laugh.

"Something funny happening between the two of you that you want to share?" I was going to get a leg cramp if I didn't move soon, so if there was something ridiculous going on that I should know about, it would really be great to hear about it so I could join in the fun.

"He said you're incredibly sexy. And that he doesn't know how I can sit here like this for so long without finding myself in trouble."

I rolled my eyes. Neither one of them had said that. I was sure of it. But if they didn't want to share, I wasn't going to push it. "It's hard to never know what people are saying. You could be making fun of me all over Paris."

Zeke pressed his nose against my neck, breathing in audibly. "I would never make fun of you to other people. Or let anyone make fun of you."

To other people? "You don't mind making fun of me yourself?"

"That's just between us. And I know, we're too quick for there to be an us. But that's the only way I do this. Fast. Quick burn. Then it's over. No one is hurt because everyone understands. I can promise you that while other things might change between us, the making fun of you won't ever."

I'd wanted his guard down, and I was pretty sure I'd gotten it. He wasn't thinking about all the reasons he shouldn't be with me right now. He was thinking about the fact that I'd been sitting in his lap for a length of time pressed up against his body.

"I just got out of a relationship that left me...very unsatisfied."

I wasn't good at this, and I was sort of winging it. Bridget always seemed to be able to get men to do what she wanted. For these moments, I was going to pretend I knew how to do this, too.

He lifted his head to whisper in my ear. "How so?"

"Kit didn't really know what he was doing. Do you?"

His laugh was low, and it moved right through me. "Young men in their early twenties never know what they're doing. That comes with experience, and getting your cock to behave and wait its turn."

I couldn't believe we were having this conversation. It was a good thing the picture was going to be in black and white, because I was sure I was red as a beet. "Zeke..."

The artist finished, effectively shutting me up before I told him I wanted him to take me back to his home and fuck me all the ways he knew how. Instead, we got up, and he paid the man as I stared at the rendition.

Pressed up against each other, we both stared at the artist in the sketch with distant eyes. Zeke looked almost angry, and I was lost. While others surrounded and complimented the work, I didn't love it. Not in the least. Was that how I appeared to strangers? With the distant, unconnected gaze that seemed like it didn't really look at anything? And Zeke, what had been making him so angry in that second?

He stepped next to me and looked down at it. "Where should we put it?"

Didn't he see what I did? Wasn't he disturbed by how we'd been captured? Apparently not. The artist took it and rolled it up, placing it in a container and handing it back to Zeke, who took it from him before he wrapped his arm around my shoulder.

Someone shrieked, and the ants crawled on my neck, rushing around like they were having a party. This one was going to be bad.

"What is it?" Zeke asked me three seconds before the teenagers arrived. They surrounded me and spoke so fast, I couldn't even guess what language they were speaking, but they knew me, and they were really excited.

It must not have been French, because Zeke didn't answer them. Instead, after a few moments of this with one of them trying to grab me and none of them taking my smile and good-natured nods to mean I didn't like what was happening, he tugged my hand and yanked me out of there, elbowing his way through the crowd.

We hustled away, eventually losing them down a small street where we darted inside the first open door we saw to wait them out. Five teenage girls. Wow. They could be pushy.

"Sorry." I sat down fast, fanning myself. My feet hadn't been up for the run, but since I'd caused it, I was hardly going to complain.

"Not your fault." He spoke to the waiter and then looked back at me. "How did it start?"

"When we were fourteen, we went out to a party. Someone was taking pictures, and we posed together. Looking back, it was sort of ridiculous that it got so much attention. We were fourteen-year-old girls, right? Bridget still had braces, Hope was wearing a headband, and I was... Well, anyway, for some reason, people really responded to that picture and we ended up in newspapers and magazines."

When he didn't respond, I kept speaking. "Then as social media did what it did, it really only got bigger, the interest in us. And Justin, of course, but it was different with him. He came out of the fascination with us. I guess we were rich, young, redheads. It was strange, but it did what it did. Eventually, we stopped fighting it."

"Sure, but they're not as interested in Hope and Bridget. Mostly you. For every hit they get, you get eight to ten more. That is substantial in the world of social media, especially exponentially."

I'd never done that math. Or listened when PR people wanted to talk to me about it. "Well, I guess it's probably because they have their shit together and I don't. I make more of an interesting look, like I might fall off a train or end up in rehab."

They placed two glasses in front of us, both filled with red wine, and then placed the bottle between us. I eyed the glasses. He did like his red wine.

And I'd liked the little bit he'd been letting me try in the last twenty-four hours.

"You hardly even drink. Unless you have a drug problem I'm missing, I don't see a trip to rehab for you happening anytime soon. You don't eat enough, but I'm not thinking you need to be hospitalized for that. You don't look sick, seem to have plenty of energy. I'm not a doctor. I'm guessing here." He sipped his wine. "And maybe you should stay off trains if you really think that is a problem."

I laughed despite myself. "So I guess it's not either of those things. I don't know why they follow me more."

"I do." He said that startling phrase right before the waiter set down cheese in front us. I almost laughed. I was in

France. I couldn't believe how long it had been for me to see cheese in France. We hadn't even had any at my rehearsal dinner because my almost mother-in-law was allergic to it. Zeke started cutting it up and distributing it on a plate for me and then some on a plate for him.

I guessed I was eating it, and the truth was that I was sort of hungry. It had been a busy morning, and I was actually hungry. And I liked cheese, a lot. Actually, the stinkier the better. I couldn't get enough of it, like other people couldn't stop eating sweets. I had that problem with dairy, so I did try to avoid it simply because it was harder to control myself.

"Aren't you going to ask me why?" He lifted his gaze to meet my own, and taking a cue from his own playbook, I winked at him, which made him grin. I loved his real smiles. They were few and far between. Zeke was more likely to smirk or fake a grin than anything else, but these real ones were like manna from heaven.

"Sure. As long as you understand I can cut up my own food. Been doing so since I was a little girl." I held up my hand. "And I'm not a little girl now. Just so we're clear."

He nodded. "Right. But if you do it, then you're going to be taking these little tiny pieces and not really eating anything."

Zeke could only say that because he didn't yet know about me and the obsession with cheese. I might take it straight off his plate and eat it if I wasn't really strict with myself. He could keep the chocolate mousse, give me brie any day of the week.

I took a bite of the goat cheese and had to close my eyes because it was so delicious. The taste exploded in my mouth. Creamy. Soft. I barely had to chew it. Before I could stop myself, I let out the smallest moan and then wished I hadn't. He'd promised not to let other people make fun of me or to make fun of me to others, but I was sure I'd just earned myself his teasing from just how much I loved that bite. I opened my lids and waited for it.

Zeke stared at me from across the table, saying nothing. There was heat in his gaze, but otherwise, I couldn't make out his thoughts. Would I ever be able to? "Why?"

He blinked. "What?"

Had he lost track of this conversation? My lunch partner shifted in his seat, leaning forward just a little bit, and took a sip of his wine. I wanted more of that goat cheese, but had to be careful about it. Too much all at once might be dangerous for my equilibrium.

"Why do they click on me more?"

His smile was slow. "Because it's impossible to stop looking at you once someone starts. You're completely intoxicating. Apparently, the way that you find that cheese."

I just had to own my dairy fixation and get it out there. There was nothing else for it but to lean into the upcoming tease. "I love dairy. I should have warned you. I can't get enough. If I have to go to rehab, it will be because I am addicted to it. Cheese is my weakness. After today, I have to ask you to not put this out in front of me again. Not if you want me to fit into the clothes you just spent a fortune on for me."

He leaned across the table, hands on both sides of it. "I would buy you ten times that amount of clothes to watch you eat that goat cheese every day just like that."

I was suddenly braver, stronger, and sexier than I had ever been. The feeling wouldn't last. I knew enough about temporary bouts of elation to understand they didn't last, but in that moment, I was queen of the fucking universe. Before I could talk myself out of it, I picked up the rest of that piece of cheese and put it right in my mouth.

The same flood of deliciousness struck me, and though I intended to keep my eyes open, I really just couldn't. It was almost sensory overload. Closing my eyes, I let it rush through me, let myself enjoy the sheer magnitude of pleasure that overtook my body in the moments it took to chew and swallow that cheese. When it was finally finished, I made myself open my eyes to meet his gaze. That was embarrassing, but somehow also filled with elation at the same time. I picked up my wine and sipped it.

In another world, where I didn't have to worry every second of the day about my sheer existence, I could have moments like this all the time. But life was hard, things were rough on everyone, and I had it pretty easy considering. Poor Layla. Poor little rich girl.

"A million different thoughts just crossed through your mind, and now you are feeling sad. How did you go from such sheer happiness to being unhappy in under five seconds flat?"

I shrugged. "I'm a lot."

"You asked me why I didn't try to get away from your dad earlier when I knew what he was doing." He was so serious in that moment, still leaning forward over the table. I wanted to look away, but made myself keep my gaze locked on his. Some things were supposed to be intense, they were meant to be. I had a gut instinct this was one of those moments.

I nodded. "I did."

"Don't picture me better than your dad. When we started out, we were very bright, very talented people, who were behind the eight ball from moment one. We didn't go to the schools our colleagues went to in high school. I was an Ivy Leaguer trying to pay for my books by serving pizza every day. Until I figured out that I could make more money betting in casinos and at the track. I was good at it."

I tried to picture that. I'd gone to those schools, wherever we lived. My father had insisted we all be educated like that, even though the constant moving made it ridiculously hard for me.

He sat back and took his wine. "We hated those boarding school fuckers." He smiled like the memory was amusing to him. "Your father had just lost your mother two years earlier when I met him. I was raising money for a defunct fund that I was keeping afloat with investors who wanted out, and I couldn't blame them. I met your dad. He was...having a bad moment at the bank where he was working."

I'd never heard any of this before. "In Chicago."

"No, by then he'd moved you to Boston. I never knew you guys in Chicago. Never knew your mom. He didn't like to talk about her, and it was almost a year of knowing him that I even knew he had four fucking children."

Now that was disappointing but not surprising. "We were always his afterthoughts."

"Not his afterthoughts. His guarded secrets." He drank more of his wine. "We all have them."

"Are you hiding a dead wife and children?"

Zeke actually laughed. "Absolutely not. No. I've fathered no offspring." He rubbed his eyes. "And grateful I haven't. Who needs that kind of leash? Wife? Kids? No."

That was funny, because I could sort of see him with a wife, with children. He liked watching sunsets. Wouldn't it be better to have someone to watch them with? He'd wanted me to see. I didn't say that because it would take us off track, and I wanted to stay right where we were.

"We made each other a promise. We'd be each other's person. Count on each other. He was a genius, I was talented. Together, we could do great things, and we did. So when it went sour, and it did, as all things do because nothing lasts forever, I didn't get out as fast as I should have. I'm decades behind in ending things, because I wanted to hold on to the idea that what we formed was real, that it could work. I sort of understood him. He was out there doing things that he shouldn't have been doing because that was his background, like it's mine. You think I don't get feeling phony in my clothes? Layla, you are looking at the king of faking it. Dress the part, and people believe you. But I learned long ago, and you'll get there some day, that we can be whoever the fuck we want to be on the inside. We can be real. However, we fake it during the day; at night, we're still our best and worst selves. Don't let the playing the part drag down the person playing it."

I supposed that was good advice. Only I hated it, and decided right then and there I wasn't going to listen to it. What was more, even though I had no business whatsoever thinking I knew anything at all, everything inside of me was screaming that Zeke shouldn't be living like that either. "What about authenticity?"

"We're pretending to date to piss off your father. What about it? Should we really be speaking about being authentic right now?"

He was right, and it killed my mood. Plummeted it right to the ground. I took another bite of my cheese, and it did nothing to make me feel better. I was a liar. I'd always been truthful. Lied to myself? Sure. I hadn't known until I absolutely did how much I hated Kit, but the second I did? I'd done something, albeit a dramatic over the top something, about it. Hell, I'd been a liar before this even started. I did it every time I went out the door dressed from head to toe in an outfit I hated just because it was expected of me. Play the part of the socialite. Or maybe it wasn't playing a part. Maybe I was lying to myself by thinking there was any chance that I could be something else.

At least if I'd married Kit, it could have continued. I'd have done what I should have, and sure, he would have been half out of his mind and inattentive, but that was what regular trips to rehab could have been for. There would have been children at some point, and despite the fact that Zeke scoffed at them, they were something I wanted more than anything. Although that could be a mistake, too.

I might be the worst mother there ever was. I had no example of one to draw on. Not even a bad one. Totally absent from my life because she took too many pills.

"Layla." His voice was low. "I..."

I waved my hand. He was right. One hundred percent that way. And he wasn't the only one who could pull off a fake smile. I was horribly good at it. But then again, I was a practiced liar. And I'd do that with Zeke until I could get on with my life, whatever that looked like. He'd made me a deal, and I'd stick to it. In the end, we'd both win.

It couldn't kill something inside of me that was already dead or had never lived to begin with.

"This is a lovely wine. You do seem to like red wine. Is that your favorite?" Benign nothing conversations were easy. I barely had to listen to his responses. I'd float away to la-la land like I always did.

"Layla." His voice was gruff, and I ignored it. Men could be managed. I'd learned that early. I just had to stay pleasant.

"Maybe when you retire, you should open a vineyard. Don't a lot of ex-businessmen do that? Not that you yourself would be out there growing the grapes. But you put your name on it. The marketing. I can really see it for you." I sipped the wine again. It was lovely. Not as fierce as the last one, but still very tasty. "Or will you be the yachting kind of retiree?"

CHAPTER ELEVEN

"**O**kay." He set down his glass with a clunk. "Normally, I'd have more wine right now because you're right, this is quite good. But I never have more than one if I'm driving my motorcycle. So you drink more, since you're playing pretend-like-you're-not-pissed-at-me. It helps."

I shrugged. "I don't know that I have any interest in being pissed at you. We might want to get the check. It's going to take me most of the afternoon to look right for tonight."

"No, it won't. You're stunning. I bet it takes you under an hour to get ready." He didn't seem thrilled to be delivering that statement by the way he spoke with his jaw clenched. "Finish your cheese. You like it. And we have a salad coming, so we're not going to be going anytime soon."

"I know I'm a liar." I couldn't leave it alone if we were going to be sitting here for some time to come. "But I had this idea that I could start over from a place of truth, and yes, it upsets me to have you pointing out that I've already failed. I'm a liar. I'll always be a liar. And I suppose I should just get over myself and move on. Is that what you'd like to hear?" I hated my tears, and after one fell, I sucked the others back in.

"Please ignore my crying. I don't like it, and I'm just over a day from having run away from my wedding. I'm not quite myself yet. I don't have my defenses in order."

He was so quiet, I wondered if he'd say anything at all. Finally, he shook his head. "Just tell me to fuck off."

"What?" I finished my cheese, barely tasting it. And the waiter came by and set down the salad.

"Tell me to fuck off. I deserve it. I ruined your lunch. I took away all that joy you had going with the cheese. Go ahead and tell me to fuck off."

I stared at him. "I don't tell people to fuck off."

"You should, you'd feel better." He took a bite of his salad. "I do think about opening a vineyard or taking over one that is failing. I do love red wine. And whisky. But I don't want to run or own a distillery. Well, maybe I could be part owner of one. Something like that. I don't want to have anything to do with the day-to-day workings."

He'd clearly thought about this, and it was distracting enough to listen to him that I took a bite of my salad and was able to taste the food without choking on all the bile our fight had brought up. "When do you see yourself doing that?"

"When I retire."

Well, that told me nothing. "You're thirty-eight. Virile. You are fit like you could win a marathon right now. I don't know your health history, and please, over lunch, don't give it to me. But you could be a billionaire, right? If you get that money my dad may have hidden somewhere. You could retire right then and there. So, this could be your second act, and it could be very soon."

"I don't know if I'll ever retire. I like working. It's what I do. I like weekends when I can take them, like today. Quick breaks to have fun, and then back at it. I think the vineyard thing will be one of many things I will do in so-called retirement. I may be even busier then than I am now."

It was really interesting how he saw his future. That wasn't how I wanted things for myself. Sure, I was too young to worry about retiring now, but in the future, I did want someone to stay with me when we were older, raise the kids together, watch them as grownups living their own lives. Laugh. Travel—assuming the other person could manage the language barrier—and have fun with.

I did want to stop.

He wanted to know what I wanted to do with my life right now, and all I could think about was what I wanted to do with it then. What did that say about me?

We finished eating and eventually made our way to his motorcycle without any interference. After putting on my helmet, he handed me the terrible sketch we'd had done, and I held on to it while we drove through traffic. I would have loved to squeeze tight to him, to put my head down on his back and close my eyes, just letting myself feel the speed and the wind. But I held on upright instead. We weren't in a real relationship. It was almost businesslike, and coworkers didn't squeeze each other intimately like that.

The ride home was so much less fun than the one there. Still, I'd spent the day in Paris, and I hadn't had a terrible time. Parts of it had been really fun, and I hadn't anticipated that at all. I'd call it a win. Small incremental steps until I figured out what to do next so I never landed in this position again were the best I could hope for.

I'd lie so that maybe someday, I could tell the truth.

Yep...it still irked me and probably would for a long while.

We got off the bike at his home and made our way inside. He stopped me when I would have turned to go into the guest room. "I have a tendency to blow things up when they're going well. Friendships. Shit like that. I had fun today. I hope you did, too."

"I did. Until lunch." Since I was trying for honesty, I let

that just come out instead of trying to shield him from hurt, which was always going to be my instinct.

"Yeah." He ran a hand through his hair. "I don't blame you on that. Tonight will probably not be a lot of laughs for you. The man I'm taking out, he's been investing with us for ten years. Your dad needs his money to keep his numbers up. He's not happy with the quarter we've had. Frankly, neither am I. But I have to keep going for now, and I have to keep him liking me so that when I split up with business, he stays with me."

I nodded. "Right. So my role is to look pretty, let the people watching think we're together, while letting you handle things the way you want to."

"Exactly." He let out a breath. Had he been worried I didn't know how these games were played? I'd watched them for a long time. If it wasn't high end finance, it was the music business, entertainment. Fashion. What did it matter? Everyone used everyone else. And right now, I was just in the middle of the deal that he had to land. Or re-land. He had to keep the deal he already had.

Like most things in life, relationships had to be managed.

Thinking of that, I took my phone out to look at my messages. "Don't worry," I didn't look at him as I spoke, "I won't embarrass you. I'll be the best little silent date you've ever had. Is he French?"

He cleared his throat. "He is, actually."

"Great. I won't even know what he's saying." I looked up after scanning my phone to see my sisters and my brother had all reached out. With as dazzling a smile as I could manage, I escaped into my room, shutting the door behind me.

I should have been more grateful than this. He was outright helping me, had given me a place to live while this got sorted, and had taken me out for fun today. I sighed. I needed to remember myself and my manners. I hardly knew this man, even if it felt like I did. I only knew what he'd shown me in a very short period of time.

It took a long time to know someone's soul.

I opened the door back up, catching him right before he stepped through his threshold. "Zeke, thank you. For everything. I can't..." I couldn't even really find the words.

He shook his head. "Don't ever thank a man like me. We take advantage of it."

I didn't know what that meant, and I decided not to think about it too hard. He could act like I had no experience dealing with intense, successful men if he wanted to. But I'd grown up surrounded by and living in the house with one.

I took off my shoes, ignored my aching feet, and stared down at my phone as I plopped down at the bed.

My first text was from Hope.

Dad is a disaster right now. Pacing around. Muttering to himself. I don't know what's going on. I got a job offer I'm thinking of taking. Oh, and how is Ezekiel Scott? He's so aloof. I can never get a read on him.

Aloof? I wouldn't use that word. Not even close to the descriptor I'd have chosen. I answered her.

Sorry you have to deal with Dad. What job offer? Zeke is good.

I usually told Hope more than that. She was great at keeping secrets, and what was more, she cared a great deal about the people in her life. But I wasn't feeling like I could open up about this. Not yet.

Maybe that was stupid. He'd kissed me once. Since then, he'd given no indication he was going to again, and he was still doing his whole "be nice to me and then turn around and insult me" thing. I didn't know how I'd explain that if I was asked to, and considering I had decided to lie to my father—and therefore my whole family—by playing a role to help Zeke, I certainly couldn't tell Hope.

She might understand, but she wouldn't approve. I didn't

think Hope had ever lied in her whole life. She was kind to a fault and yet still always managed to tell the truth.

What was I going to say? Gee, Hope, I'm engaging in something that is going to hurt Dad in some passive-aggressive maneuvering because Zeke is going to help me get control of my life? Oh, forget the passive part. It was aggressive-aggressive.

Yep, I was going to be silent on this. And continue to hate myself over it. I rolled onto my back and read Bridget's message.

I hate men. Let's never get married. Let's be strange old ladies living in the Hamptons together. We can talk to cats and garden.

I grinned. What was going on with her? *What's going on? And Kit is the one who has to be mad. I did the leaving.*

Oh, I've just been in love with the same man practically my whole life, and he couldn't care less that I exist. No big deal. Ignore me, I'm drinking.

She was? That would mean Bridget was day drinking, and I'd never seen her do that. Plus, it looked like we had more in common than even I knew. *When I get back home, we can get started on that whole gardening thing. I can't say that I've ever touched a plant. Have you?*

I finally made myself look at Justin's text. *Are you just going to ignore me? Fucking answer me. Are you alive? Dead? I mean wtf? Why can't you answer me? Like you've never done something wrong? Why are you such a holier than thou bitch?*

Okay. I read it once and then a second time. Justin had never spoken to me like that ever. And he'd left me with no money in the middle of a place where I couldn't speak the language. How had I become the holier than thou bitch?

I grabbed a pillow and smacked the bed with it. Once and then again. And then a third fucking time. There were times in life that I just had to beat the shit out of something, and my pillow always served that purpose. Oh, my dad had forgotten to include me on birthday flowers he'd sent to Hope and Bridget because it had been an oversight. No problem. I'd beat the hell out of my pillow. Justin totally screws me over and makes it my fault in exactly one day? Sure. Zeke's guest room pillow would have to do.

My phone dinged, and I looked down at it expecting Bridget to have answered the gardening question. Only it wasn't her. Kit had finally responded.

There he was in a picture with two beautiful women, one under each arm, both of them topless. He was in Bali. I recognized the pink and blue roof. Oh wow. He'd gone on our honeymoon. Well, good for him. Someone should be using the room. And the one on the right had really big nipples. Were they real?

But it was the words he'd sent with it that made me feel cold, not the accompanying photo. *Drop dead bitch.*

Twice in one day I'd been called a bitch. Maybe they were on to something, and I just didn't know it.

I bit my lip to stop the tears that threatened and went to take a shower. I'd just get busy getting beautiful. If I were a bitch, and Kit had every right to call me that even if Justin didn't, then I'd be a pretty one.

Halfway to the bathroom, I stopped. This was like a bandage I needed to rip off. I hadn't checked social media, which had to make me the worst so-called influencer there ever was. I opened up my Instagram and started to take a look. It took almost no time to find myself. There I was, everywhere.

Most of the shots were of me running in my wedding gown. I'd left it in the closet but now I wanted to slash it to pieces. I scanned through fast. Swipe. Swipe. Swipe. Was there anything else? Why yes, there I was with Zeke. In the café helping Renee. Talking to Isobel. I hadn't been wrong, the ants on the back of my neck had told me I was being watched and photographed. And then it went on. Someone had gotten us in Montmartre getting our sketch done. They hadn't bothered us and there was only one. The final one was us running before we went to eat.

Sure, there were real paparazzi all over, but anyone with a cell phone and an interest could do the same. Every human being was on display to every other human being at all times. It could have been worse. Or at least I thought that, until I found Amanda Hill. Gossip vlogger extraordinaire. She had been really invested in my wedding and even more so in the demise of it. Oh, she had a ton of things to say about me and none of them were kind. Ugly. Not worth Kit's time. Has been. Of course, that implied I had ever been, and I wasn't sure that could be exactly. Stupid.

I threw my phone down on the bed. I hoped we could pull off something tonight, because if Zeke wanted our photos to make my dad mad, he was going to have to hope anything could be more interesting than me running like a mad woman through the streets of Paris in a wedding dress that was beautiful and yet the most ugly thing I'd ever seen.

Or maybe it just showed my soul through its white fabric. The darkness of my worthlessness seeping through for the world to see.

That wasn't helpful. It was a stranger saying that about me, and she was fickle. One second, she loved me, the next, Kit. Hell, I knew how this worked. She loved whoever it got her more views to love.

And Kit was entitled. I'd run out on our wedding.

And Justin...well, that one hurt. We'd never been close, but that was my brother. I put on the water, as hot as I could make it. I was going to scald these thoughts away.

Maybe it wasn't Justin. Maybe somewhere inside of him was the sweet, quiet boy who drew as well as my mother did, who sang to himself, and who had smiled when he ate his eggs in the morning. Somewhere, that person still had to exist.

I'd thought I saw him for half a second yesterday when he'd offered to help me.

But of course, that had been fake.

I put my head under the water, and I let the hot water run over me. There would come a time when I wouldn't have to put up with this. I would have a life that didn't involve one second of what other people thought of me.

Somehow.

I blew my hair straight. It was a very severe look for me. Most of the time, I embraced the waves or curls, depending on the mood my hair was in that day. But I wrangled it straight and stared in the mirror at the look. I thought that Bridget and I looked less like each other than we both resembled Hope. Like this, however, the resemblance between Bridget and me was striking.

Most people would think I was crazy to have those thoughts. We all looked alike, so much so that strangers sometimes couldn't tell us apart.

I applied my makeup darker than I'd wear on a regular basis.

My underwear and bra matched, a must have for me, and were nude so that no one could see it through the dress I was going to clothe myself in.

I grabbed it off the hanger in the closet. Someone had hung it up while we'd been out. The barely-there staff that Zeke preferred not to see too often.

I'd never wear anything shorter than it, but I'd looked up the club we were going to and sexy was the name of the game at this place. I didn't want to look like I couldn't keep up.

The dress was gold, sparkly, and the saleswoman had called it a mini dress. That was a good description. If it hadn't had thick straps on it, I'd have had to go without a bra. My breasts were just at the mid-way point where sometimes I could get away with it and sometimes I couldn't. It really depended on the dress, and lately, I only wanted to wear things that I could wear a regular supportive bra with. The bra I had on pushed my cleavage up enough that it poked through the round neckline of the dress, making me look bustier than I actually was.

I strapped on some barely-there gold shoes which were going to hurt, and I had to hope no one looked at my feet too closely. They wrapped around my ankle with the tiniest little heel that would give me a little boost, but not enough to make it so I couldn't walk in them. As it was, my feet were going to hurt even more later. I might be hobbling tomorrow.

With a quick look in the mirror, I decided I looked good enough to pull this off. I never looked very long in the mirror if I could help it. But I had to help Zeke with this deal we had made, and that meant trying my best to make people— well, my father—believe it.

I snapped a photo of myself, hand on my hip, bored look in my eyes. Posting it fast, I wrote a caption that would get attention.

Sometimes life throws you lemons. And sometimes it throws you pretty gold dresses that you get to wear out with the man you've been lusting after since you were too young to do so. XO—Layla

I put it out there and headed to find Zeke. He stood at the bottom of the stairs, and I caught my breath looking at him. I should have known he'd look like a million dollars. Zeke didn't grow up with the right clothes to look like he had money, but he'd clearly hired a better stylist than he had a decorator, because he didn't ever look anything except exactly right. And gorgeous in the effect.

He wore dark denim pants, almost black but not quite. He didn't have socks but expensive loafers that made him look casual. The pants were tight and well-fitting, showing off how muscular his legs were. The belt he'd slipped into was fashionable not necessity. The man would have no problems keeping up his pants. They were practically painted on his legs. The belt was a light brown that matched the light khaki jacket he'd put over a white dress shirt that he had unbuttoned to the top of his chest.

Fuck me, he was really, really handsome. He looked up from his phone as I came down the stairs, his eyes widening as he took me in.

I wanted to be complimented, to think that his gaze was because he approved of the outfit I'd picked out. Redheads didn't always wear gold. Everyone had opinions. We shouldn't wear yellow or gold or red or pink. But I believed anyone could wear anything as long as they felt happy in the outfit.

So I pretended to be joyful in whatever I wore and called it a day.

But his gaze might have meant he didn't approve. He might be getting ready to say something shitty, in which case, I had to have my guard up and my I-didn't-care attitude ready to go.

"Wow." He put his phone in his jacket pocket and extended his hand for me to take it. "Layla, you look...incredible. Every guy in there is going to want to fuck you tonight."

Not the compliment I would have hoped for, but not the worst either. "That was the idea. To make them notice that I'm with you. I guess mission accomplished. I posted to try to get us some attention. I don't usually, but for this, I made the exception. We're not going on your motorcycle, right? I'm not sure I could straddle it in this outfit."

He squeezed my hand. "No, princess. We're getting

driven. Neither one of us is going to worry about driving tonight."

"I can't drive." I shrugged. "But I guess I could try in an emergency."

"We have a driver. So no emergency, and if you want to learn to drive, I can teach you."

Maybe someday I'd learn, but I doubted it would be from Zeke. "Oh, I forgot my phone. Hold on." I turned and rushed as best I could in the shoes I was in back up the stairs, where I grabbed my phone and purse. I had my wallet in the purse —not that I had any money—and then went back downstairs.

"All set."

He put his hand around the back of my neck and drew me to him. "Are your feet all right in those shoes?"

"I suffer for beauty. I'll be fine." I smiled at him. "You look incredible, by the way. Every woman in there is going to wish they were me tonight."

He narrowed his eyes. "That's a better compliment than the one I gave you."

"Yes." I grinned at him. "But that's okay. You can't be good at everything. So if you happen to be bad at telling a girl that she looks pretty after she spent hours getting ready, then so be it. You'll have to take the loss on that one."

He rewarded me with one of his rare real smiles. "You don't look pretty. You look beautiful. Hot. Sexy. And I meant what I said. Every man is going to want to fuck you. But they won't get to. Want to know why?"

I swallowed. The answer was easy. Because I was pretending to be there with him. Still, I asked. "Why?"

"They won't dare to try when they know you're with me."

That shouldn't have been sexy. Only it was.

CHAPTER TWELVE

We had photographs taken of us on the way into the club. Real paparazzi snapped us and called out my name. Within minutes, they knew Zeke's, too. I held his hand and smiled. Zeke was stiff. He'd thought he wanted this, but maybe he hadn't understood what it would really entail. Amanda the vlogger would be talking about him within the hour if she weren't already, since I'd posted my fake happy picture.

When we finally got inside, the music was loud, which was to be expected, and it made me clench my teeth. I hated these places. I didn't dance well, didn't want to, and it was all about everyone staring at everyone else, no matter what country you were in.

But that was what Zeke had wanted tonight. So I plastered my best socialite smile, shook hands with the man Zeke was meeting, who looked at me like I was the best piece of meat he'd ever seen, and sat down to spend the night being quiet and saying nothing to anyone.

I guessed the idea of these places was to be with the best-looking guy in the room. I certainly was. All eyes were on us, and phones were out aplenty. I leaned a little closer to him so they could take a better picture.

He wasn't paying attention. Zeke had gone into sales mode, and since they were speaking French, he could have been selling me to the man—whose name was Luc—for all that I knew. Maybe I should hire a translator. I chewed on my lower lip and then stopped. That was a terrible habit. This could actually be the year that I beat back some of my bad habits.

A waiter came by, since we had table service, and dropped off food and very expensive champagne. As I knew this wasn't Zeke's preference of alcohol, it must have to do with Luc. My pretend boyfriend—could I really call him a boyfriend if he was thirty-eight years old?—leaned over to me. "I have no idea if any of this food is good. We should have eaten before we got here."

I took a sip of my champagne. "I'm sure this is fine. This is France. It's all good food, right?"

He elbowed me gently. "You doing okay?"

I was bored and the evening had hardly gotten started. But, yes, I supposed I was fine. "Sure. I might go wander around soon."

Zeke nodded. "Don't trip and fall."

I smirked at him. "Thanks. I've been walking on my own for some time now."

He leaned back in his seat, ignoring me now to listen to something Luc was saying. I had been trying all night to figure out who Luc was exactly. I could google him, but this was a lot more fun when it came down to it. Small details explained the man. Zeke always wore the same watch. What did that tell me? He valued it. He didn't discard things when they got old, and he took care of what belonged to him. I didn't know him well yet, but I could tell already those things were true.

Why else would he have held on to this relationship with my father for so long? And here he was still trying to. Until they separated, the efforts he made today would benefit a man he didn't like.

He smirked at something Luc said, giving off an entirely different appearance than the seconds before. Zeke could also be mean when he wanted to, and I'd bet a real adversary I didn't want to mess with if I found myself at odds with him at some point. I hoped that never happened.

The thought made my stomach clench. I knew next to nothing about him when it came down to it. Although, he'd told me a secret, a big one, and when he pushed my buttons, he also seemed inclined to give me leverage over him, too. He was such a mixture of things, it was hard to understand him, even by examining his accessories.

Suddenly, it was as though the music was too loud and the seat uncomfortable. I needed a moment. These sorts of sensations were familiar to me, but I was more accustomed to them on airplanes. I rose, catching both Zeke and Luc's attention.

I smiled. "I'm going to the ladies' room."

Without pausing, I left them sitting there. They wouldn't even miss me. In fact, I could sneak out the back, grab a ride share, and be back at Zeke's house for all that it mattered. We'd performed our function and been seen together. I might even suggest I do that when I got back from the bathroom.

This club used too much strobe light. It was a mistake I saw far too often. The clubgoers didn't like it overdone when it came down to it. Not that anyone was asking me what I thought. I could just see how it put off at least three quarters of the dancers when it went on too long. Some places it worked, but here, people wanted to see and be seen. The strobes got in the way. Maybe it was that the manager didn't understand what he had here. He thought he had a dance club, or perhaps that was what the owners wanted. I didn't know and didn't care. I just knew that I hated strobes. They made my eyes hurt.

The hallway to the bathroom was full, but I managed to not fall into anyone as I made my way inside. I didn't actually have to pee, which was helpful because the stalls were all taken up, but there was space by one of the mirrors, and I stared at myself for a long moment, forcing myself to breathe.

My strange panic-induced need to move was probably not as bizarre as I thought it was. I'd run from my wedding. I was bound to have some delayed reactions. Maybe I should go ahead and talk to a therapist. I was probably way overdue for talking to one anyway.

"And I thought he was coming here with me, but he came with her."

A girl cried out in accented English, weeping onto her friend's shoulder in the space next to me on the wall of mirrors.

I looked up, startled by the sound. Other than Zeke, I hadn't heard English spoken aloud until I said it since I'd run from my wedding. People responded in English after they realized I couldn't speak French. But those two were, if I had to guess, Irish...and they were crying in the bathroom. Well, one of them was and the other was consoling her.

That's what friends did. Or sisters when they weren't handling our father.

They saw me staring. I saw it the second they recognized me, which in this case was a good thing, since otherwise, they'd probably have told me to go fuck myself for so rudely watching them and listening in on their conversation.

I quickly looked down and spoke to them even though I stared at the sink. "Sorry, you were speaking my language. It caught my attention. I'm not trying to be invasive." I looked up to smile. "But if someone did that to you, they're out of their mind because you're gorgeous. And he's not worth your tears."

I'd managed to get the attention of all the women in the bathroom who were speaking in hushed voices. I ignored them since I couldn't understand them to begin with, which made it significantly easier to do.

The crying woman brushed tears off her face. "You really are her."

I shrugged. "The redhead who ran from her wedding? Yes. Whoever it is out there who treated you so disrespectfully, he is going to swallow his tongue when I'm done with you, if you want."

They stared at each other and then back at me. I had them. I could fix her up and make her already stunning black outfit look even sexier when she walked out of this bathroom. I should probably mind my own business when faced with these situations, and it wasn't like I ran around New York City fixing outfits on a regular basis. But it wasn't like I was terribly busy either. I could go sit in silence with Zeke, or help this poor woman make some man eat his bad attitude.

She took my hand in hers. "This is so surreal. You're here."

I wanted to shrink from her touch. This part of the role I tried to play was hard for me. Truth was I was happier not being around too many people all at once. The bathroom was getting crowded, and I had no security to help me. I steeled my back. I'd been the one to open this proverbial door, I was going to figure out how to make this okay.

"Where's your makeup bag?"

It didn't take long to make the blonde beauty feel better about herself. Sometimes, it wasn't about what I actually did as much as the fact that I told them they looked gorgeous and they believed me. We took a couple of selfies together, and I did my best to seem like the Layla they wanted me to be. I slightly adjusted the belt on her dress and made her change earrings with her friend.

In the meantime, they talked. They were from Cork, Ireland. I'd never been there, but I was now invited to visit, even though I couldn't remember their first names, and they wanted me to stay with them. I did a lot of nodding and smiling.

When I was finished, the no-longer-crying one of the pair exited the bathroom with her head held high, looking like she'd just come off a runway. I followed fast behind her lest I found myself having to makeover everyone in the bathroom. I was happy to be helpful, but the encounter was draining, even if it was my own fault.

The crowd in the hallway had doubled, too. Women whispered and some tried to grab me. I dodged and weaved until a tall man with blond hair stood right in front of me. "Hi," he said in English and sounded American. He didn't have any discernible accent to me at all, but I was sure people from other countries would think that he did.

I looked up to meet his blue eyes, which were red-rimmed. I knew the look well because I'd just left someone with similarly rimmed eyes at the altar. This guy was on something, and I really wasn't in the mood. "Hi."

Having said that, I intended to move around him, but he didn't budge. In fact, he grabbed on to my arms. "I heard you were here. I know your brother. We went to school together. Well, for a year before you guys moved out of San Francisco. How is he?"

"Fine. I'll tell him you said hi." Not that I'd taken his name or was in any way going to speak to Justin anytime soon, but maybe he wouldn't notice.

"What's your hurry? Let's dance. And then you can tell me all about Justin and what that—"

"Sorry." Zeke's arm was suddenly around me. I hadn't even

seen him come up, let alone get close enough to me to put his arm around my waist, but I was grateful for it just the same. I sighed. His presence was...comforting. "She only dances with me."

With that statement, he moved his arm from my waist to my hand, wrapped our fingers together, and tugged me with him so that no one in the club was getting near me anytime soon. I expected him to take me back to Luc and our seats, but instead, we were on the dance floor.

The strobe lights burned but only for a second before I forgot they were happening at all. I didn't see Luc anywhere, and Zeke's hold on me was intense as we moved to the music. I was no kind of dancer, but I didn't care. He was holding me like he owned me.

And he could actually dance. His muscles were hard under my hands, and I held on to him like the lifeline he had suddenly become. Dancing was a prequel, an invitation to check out how the person you were with moved in intimate ways. My body buzzed being this close to his in a way that was different than it had been on his motorcycle. My breasts ached and pushed against his chest.

Was this real? Or was he posing for some cameras somewhere? I didn't care. I'd pretend this was real. If it were all fake, that would just make for a better screenshot later. I threw myself into the moment. The beat. The way that the crowd was around us, all of them lost in whatever they were doing at that very second. Nothing existed except right fucking then.

His mouth came down on mine. Like before, I hadn't known he was going to kiss me, but I didn't mind it in the least. This time, I kissed him back. It was hard to chase where he led. He kissed differently than I'd ever been before. We weren't doing this together; it felt more like he claimed me, and I was to come along into his passion because he demanded it. I loved the sensation.

Finally, he pulled back and stared down at me, his hand coming to pinch the tip of my chin. Bending over, he whisper-shouted in my ear to make himself heard over the bass of the music. Or maybe it was the pounding of my heart. "You vanished into that bathroom for a fucking hour." Had it been that long? "I might have thought something happened to you if I hadn't heard the whole place start to buzz about how you were helping some girl in the bathroom. Don't do that again."

I lifted my chin, which made him move his fingers. "Did you kiss me as some sort of punishment?"

"I kissed you because I wanted to. I always do what I want." He bit my earlobe, and I yelped but not in pain. No, I was absolutely stunned by the way my knees threatened to give out and pleasure surged right to my core. I'd had no idea I would have liked that, but I really, really did.

He smiled. I couldn't see it, but somehow, I could feel it. I knew deep in my soul that in that moment, he was absolutely grinning against my ear. His own breath hitched. "And you don't feel punished right now. Come on. Fun's over. Let's go home."

I had to think. My mind whirled, and it was like I was in a fog I couldn't clear. "What about Luc?"

"I sent him off with a hooker half an hour ago."

Well...that was one way to show the man a good time.

Back at his monstrous house, the kiss and the bite might as well have never happened. Zeke's stiff-backed reserved presence returned. My stomach grumbled. I'd never eaten the food. It was really amazing. Most of the time, I wasn't even aware when I was hungry, but since he'd started insisting on my eating, it was as though my hunger instinct returned in a major way.

He nodded at the guard, who was a different person than the one I'd seen the other times we'd come and gone, and entered the house. Without turning to me, Zeke strode to the kitchen. "You're hungry."

Yep...he'd heard my stomach rumble. "I am."

He flung open the fridge. "Usually Carlos leaves me something to eat. Apparently not tonight."

"That's fine." I walked past him. "I'll make us something to eat."

Zeke jolted, turning to look at me. "You can cook?"

"Not like your chef, but I can put something together. How about comfort food? Hmm?" I took his place by the fridge. Yes, it was fully stocked. I wasn't going to have to try hard to make this happen. "Go sit down."

He pulled out a chair at the counter and did as I asked. "I wouldn't have thought of you as being able to cook."

"Again, don't get your hopes up for some kind of gourmet thing here. I am going to grill some chicken and cook up some vegetables. Most of the time, I prefer to eat at home. Easier to control the caloric intake. Speaking of which, do you think we could get me a scale?"

He was quiet for a moment. "No, you can use the one in my bathroom if you want one. I'm not giving you your own scale."

Was he serious? I'd no sooner placed the chicken on the pan to quickly grill it on the stovetop when he made that announcement. I looked over my shoulder at him. "Why not?"

"Because I like you eating three times a day, and I have a very good idea that it's going to stop if I give you too much access to a scale. So, you can use mine. I'll keep an eye on it."

I groaned. "Do I have enough money in my account to buy my own fucking scale?"

"You do. But if you put that in the house, I'm going to throw it out, so ask yourself how much you want that scale because you'll have to buy it again and again."

I momentarily considered throwing the chicken at him. Instead, I took a long breath. "My feet held up tonight. Maybe we could run tomorrow."

I didn't exercise enough. The sad truth was I could eat more if I took the time to work out. And if he thought I wasn't going to go into his bathroom just as much as I fucking wanted to in order to use his scale, he had another think coming. I absolutely would. In fact, I might go in there and weigh myself ten times as much as I usually would just for the sheer fact of pissing him off.

I smirked. That was a whole side of my personality I hadn't experienced lately. A little bit obstinate...

"I'll wake you when I get up and we can run."

I nodded. "Sounds good, but I might already be up."

I cooked in silence, but it didn't feel strained. Instead, I was fully aware of his eyes on me and not in the way I was when others were viewing my every move. It wasn't the creepy ants crawling on my neck. No, it was warm, like he stroked me with his gaze. Still, when I turned around, he was quiet and remote as though that hadn't happened.

Our late dinner done, I served us and dug in when he did. I'd done a good job. The chicken wasn't dry, and although it was simple and not anything special, I liked eating it. Most of the time when I prepared a meal, it was just for me.

He rose after a moment and poured us both a glass of red wine from a bottle he'd had corked in the fridge. I took a sip, and he lifted his eyebrow. "Like that one?"

"It's robust." That seemed the right word. "Yes, I like it."

"That's one I might buy. That vineyard. We'll see." He

drummed his fingers on the table. "I have to work tomorrow. My day starts around noon here and goes late."

That made sense with the time changes. "That's how you go to that café every morning. You start later."

"Yep." He took another long sip. "And we'll start to work on what-will-Layla-do-with-her-life tomorrow, too."

"Great." I rolled my eyes, and he laughed, throwing his head back. I loved the sound and the way he did that so easily. This was the real Zeke. Not the way he'd been with Luc. That was a show.

He grabbed my plate when I was done and put it with his in the sink. I guessed it would sit there until morning. I finished my wine which made my head feel heavy. It was late, and the wine had made me warm.

But I wasn't sleepy.

We walked together upstairs, and I paused outside of the room. "Does the television work in my room?"

"It should. Why? Did it not?" He strode toward me and opened my door before entering. At that point, he discovered what I had when I looked for it during the time I got dressed earlier. There was no remote anywhere I could find, and the TV didn't easily turn on.

He sighed, loudly. "I pay them a lot of money to not have this problem. It'll be fixed tomorrow. It's just an oversight. Come on, you can watch TV in my room." Like he'd simply solved the problem, he strode down the hallway back to his own suites.

I blinked. "I don't want to put you out."

"You're not. I can't sleep yet either. Wound up. Get changed and come in. You can pick what we watch."

It was very easy to follow his directions, and I decided not to question why that was. I changed into my pajamas, which were a small pair of boy shorts and a white tank top, and went into his bedroom. The remote was on his bed, displayed obviously in the center. Which side was I supposed to sit on?

Zeke exited the bathroom, shirtless and in dark pajama pants. Once again, I couldn't seem to help but stare at just how buff he was. My cheeks heated up. I'd been up against him on the dance floor. What was wrong with me now that I'd suddenly reverted to being utterly stunned at the sight of him shirtless?

He sat down on the left side and patted the right. Both of us sat on top of his comforter. Did he just want me to put the TV on? "I can totally go back to my room. This is your private time."

"Layla. I told you it was fine, so it's fine. End of story." He handed me the remote. "Whatever you want to watch, put it on."

I flipped through streaming services until I landed on *Star Trek*. It was a secret I didn't often discuss, but I was absolutely a huge science fiction fan. One of my nannies had shared her love of it with me when I was about nine years old. I'd been hooked ever since.

"Picard or Kirk?" He crossed his arms over his chest.

I grinned. "Could be Janeway or Sisko, right? Or Archer."

He shook his head. "I'll ask it again. Picard or Kirk?"

"Picard was the captain who hooked me, and I have come to love Kirk."

Zeke smirked at me. "Good answer."

I put it on. I guessed we'd start with episode one on the *Next Generation*. "Encounter at Farpoint" was a famous one. I knew it well and even though it was totally bizarre to be in Zeke's bed watching it, there was a familiarity to it that soon lulled me into forgetting about the oddness and just loving the moment. At the very least, I'd never forget this.

CHAPTER THIRTEEN

We watched three episodes and had started on the fourth when I fell asleep. I didn't remember doing that or even know I was about to. One second, I was wide awake, the next thing I knew, I was being gently scooted over so Zeke could cover me with the blanket. I roused enough to realize what was happening.

"Sorry." I struggled to sit up. "I didn't mean to..."

"Stop. Go back to sleep. You're fine."

That didn't make sense. "In your bed..."

"Yes, back to sleep." The room was dark, and I was warm. He told me it was okay, and so it must be. Zeke never did anything he didn't want to do. He'd kick me out if he wanted me to go. I really hoped I didn't snore. That was the last thing I could think about, because dreaming was just such a nice place to go.

It was cold, and that brought me back at some point from the cushion of happiness where I had been cocooned. But there was warmth nearby, like a beacon, and I rolled toward it snuggling back down.

I woke up when the sun came through the window, hitting

me in the eyes. It was morning. That much I knew. I had to wake up and do...something. Morning meant getting out of bed.

Wrenching my eyes open, I was suddenly very confused. Where was I? It took half a second to come back to me. I'd fallen asleep in Zeke's bed, and what was more was that I was half sprawled on him. My arm was across his chest and my head sort of pressed into his side, or it had been before I lifted it.

He was on his back, one arm under my body, the other above his head slightly touching the back of the bed. His eyes were closed. In sleep, Zeke looked the most relaxed I'd ever seen him. He had incredibly long eyelashes, longer than my own, and I coveted them.

Zeke was a quiet sleeper. I couldn't hear his intakes and exhales of breath, even as I watched his chest move and could feel it under my hand. I should let go of him, immediately. He'd let me stay because I'd fallen asleep, and here I was, grasping on to him like a lifeline in sleep. I'd totally invaded his space.

I let go of him and rolled over to where I should have been on my side of the bed. He made a sound and turned on his side, his arm swinging over me before he tugged me against him, this time his nose in my hair.

I lay there not moving. Well...that had just happened.

I'd tried to give him back his space, and he hadn't wanted to let go. I supposed I could force the issue, wrench myself away and leave the bed. He'd probably prefer it when he woke up and saw how we were. Sure, we'd had two instances of him kissing—and once biting me—together. But it was always like it hadn't happened afterwards, and it wasn't because I didn't want to talk about it.

It was just that I didn't know what to say. How did you address the subject? Hey, remember when you bit my ear? I was suddenly more turned on than I'd ever been, and then you acted like it didn't happen...

Plus, now there was this moment. I'd never been held, that I could remember. Certainly not by...

He sucked in a long breath and let go of me, rolling onto his back. I quickly shut my eyes. Yes, I would pretend to be asleep. Then I could spare us having to talk about this when we were already so good at acting like nothing happened when clearly things did.

"Sorry." His voice sounded sort of rougher than it usually did. It was an intimate moment. The kind where I would now know he woke up sounding like that in the morning. "You don't have to pretend to sleep. I know you're up. That little snore you do when you're sleeping? It's a sure-fire tell."

I rolled over, opening my eyes. "I don't snore."

"You do. But it's not bad, I kind of like it, actually. Not a bad sound, just a constant reminder you're in the room." He sat up all the way, and the blanket fell off his waist. Didn't he get cold in here? My room hadn't been like this, but it was as though he kept this room like it was a refrigerator.

"I'm sorry if I kept you up." Both Hope and Bridget snored. It wouldn't surprise me if I did, too.

"You didn't." He looked me over for a long second, long enough that my cheeks heated up from the way he appraised me. I might look like hell. It was morning, and I hadn't looked in a mirror yet. My entire appearance could be a disaster.

I sat up, deciding to act like I didn't care. He reached over, pushing my hair out of my eyes. "Layla, you know that I don't do serious. I've made that clear enough I think, but let me be explicit just in case. I don't do relationships or dating. What we're doing out there is pretend. What may or may not be going on here between us, it won't ever be anything serious."

"We're lying here in your bed, having done nothing to earn this morning after speech, and you want to talk about how you'll never have feelings for me? Fine. I ran out on my wedding. I don't think I'm a pillar of relationship strength either."

Zeke squeezed my cheek in his palm. "Well, I wouldn't say that we did nothing. You have a mark on your ear from me, and I'm not usually a biter, but you inspired me." He winked at me. "Just as long as you understand this up front. I don't worry about it usually. The women I see..."

I held up my hand, my stomach turning slightly. "Don't tell me about your other women, or I'm going to worry that I have to get treated for a disease for having lain here."

He laughed. "I don't bring people here. I told you that. I don't even have guests. You're perfectly safe on all fronts. The point is you're very young, and I don't want stars in your eyes."

Now it was my turn to laugh. "Do I find you sexy? Yes. I have eyes, but they don't have stars in them. We could have meaningless sex right now. Is that what you want to do?"

He shook his head, slowly. "No. I absolutely do not." Zeke got out of bed. "Come on. Let's go run."

I'd just offered him sex, and he'd turned me down. I opened and closed my mouth. Embarrassment flooded me, and I wondered if I could go and hide under his covers, never coming out again. Why had I done that? I put my head in my hands, and I counted to ten. Maybe I could stop dying of embarrassment after I reached that number. One. Two.

"Layla?" I lifted my head out of my hands to stare at him, forcing myself to meet his gaze because I wouldn't add coward to idiot on the list of things I'd managed to be before breakfast that morning.

"Yes?" I put my hands in my lap, since I had to do something with them.

"Coming?" He tilted his head. Zeke had already managed to get his shorts on and was going into the closet to get his sneakers, or that was what I would assume.

I nodded. "Yes. On my way."

I threw the blanket off myself and tried to ignore the fact that he smirked at me on my way out of the room. He was ridiculously handsome with that smirk on his face, and I hated that I thought that. Why did he have to be so confusing? Hadn't that whole conversation he'd had with me upon waking been about his wanting to have sex with me? How could I possibly have misinterpreted that?

He wanted meaningless sex, and I'd offered it to him.

Men in general were confusing as hell, and Zeke was the worst of them. Seriously.

I was a terrible runner. When he'd suggested we run together, I somehow had assumed the man used a treadmill. Why had I thought that? I wasn't sure, but I was definitely wrong. Joints aching from running on pavement wrong. I also had almost no stamina or ability to keep up with him, and yet I kept pushing.

Maybe if I had more practice running, my rush down the aisle away from Kit would have been more graceful, or I would have been able to do it whilst keeping my shoes on at the same time. Women did it in movies all the time. They ran in heels. I couldn't seem to do it very well in my sneakers.

I'd always been able to maintain my weight by not eating very much, and the ability to do that had meant that I didn't focus very much on getting into shape. Maybe that was why Zeke didn't want to sleep with me. Maybe he didn't like how my body looked.

I gritted my teeth. That wasn't helpful. The trouble with

running outside was that however far I went I had to get back. And Zeke wasn't showing any signs of stopping. I could see the back of his head as he ran a distance ahead of me. I hadn't exactly expected him to slow down to wait, but I would have liked the ability to throw my hands in the air and say no more, with him actually being able to hear me do so.

Ants crawled on my neck, and I quit walking. They weren't really ants. I pretty much had to remind myself of that every time it happened. It just meant someone was staring at me intently. I turned around, half-expecting to see people with phones but there was no one there. Just the occasional car driving down the street, and no one seemed all that interested in me.

I had to catch my breath, which meant I was turning around and slowly making my way back to Zeke's house. I was pretty sure I knew the way, and I had my phone in my pocket if I did get lost.

I loved it when fashion designers put pockets in things. As human beings, we really did need them most of the time.

Across the street was a painting on the wall of a gray building that seemed like it didn't belong there. It caught my attention, and despite the fact that I was currently showering the ground with my sweat and sounded like I was about to drop dead from how fast I breathed, I crossed the street the first chance it was safe and went to look at it. A clown. That's what it was. Someone had decorated the wall with the face of a sad clown. It was really cool. The eyes seemed to follow me.

A woman rounded the corner and stopped to look at it as I did. She had long black hair and she wore a purple jumpsuit. I'd never seen one before. The whole look made me smile. I loved when things were unique. There were so few times in life when I could really say I saw something new.

And I was only twenty-two. That seemed too young to be so sour.

She said something to me, and I steeled myself to respond. "I'm sorry. I don't speak French."

"Ah, yes, you don't speak French. Are you American? Didn't learn it?"

I rubbed the back of my neck. I could say unequivocally that for the first time in a while, this woman I'd run into on the street had no idea who I was. I was just a strange American to her who didn't speak her language.

That was sort of...fun. "Right. They didn't teach it in school. I'd like to know it."

She pointed at the clown. "You like it?"

"I do. He caught my attention. I...I guess he seems very different than anything else I've seen in a while."

She shrugged. "I find him repulsive."

"Repulsive?" Now that was a strong word. "Why do you find him repulsive?"

"Clowns."

I wanted to laugh, but I kept myself together. Some people did have a clown thing, and it was real. I wasn't going to laugh at her. I was pretty sure that she could kick my butt if she wanted to. Even in the purple jumpsuit that looked like it was circa 1990, she was pretty badass.

"Clowns can be very off putting. Do you know who painted this?"

"No." She shook her head. "They're popping up all over town. It is a thing now. And the fact that you like it tells me that you have terrible taste."

I nodded. "Yes, you're right. I have terrible taste."

I walked a bit to the right to look more at the clown. He had sad eyes. The more I stared at them, the more that was obvious to me. I'd be the girl who had terrible taste for a bit. That might be a fucking relief.

I just wondered if the person who painted this clown had wanted to say something about how we see things.

I looked over at the purple girl. "My mother was a painter."

"Yes?" She pushed her hair over her shoulder. "Did she have any success?"

"Her name was Meredith Scott." I couldn't remember the last time I'd spoken her name. It was as though sometimes you put words away so deep inside a box labeled "do not say" that the next time you actually had to utter them, they were hard to form on your tongue. Or maybe it was just me.

Her mouth fell open. "Your mother was Meredith Scott?"

I knew then as she stared at me that she understood a lot about art and something more, it hadn't been an accident that she came out here to talk about this painting. Artists were a rare breed. I'd only ever observed them from afar, and she was way too invested in talking about this clown with a stranger to truly hate this painting.

"This painting you did of this clown is brilliant. Haunting. Not awful at all. And I'll never forget it."

"Layla." Zeke yelled my name as he ran around the corner. "There you are. When did I lose you?"

I didn't turn to look at him but kept my eyes on the purple artist. "Yes, my mother was Meredith Scott. And you are really talented. I have great taste."

She grinned at me, her first real smile, and only then did I turn to Zeke. He was gorgeous and sweaty. Immediately, I remembered he'd turned me down that morning when I'd offered him sex.

"You didn't have to come back for me; I was going home. I just met..." I motioned toward where the artist should be, but she rounded the corner and was gone. "That person. And I stopped to talk about this clown."

He stared at her and then me. "That was the purple dabbler, wasn't it?"

"Who?" Okay, I wasn't going to notice how his muscles were things of beauty. Men shouldn't get to be so gorgeous.

"The purple dabbler. An artist is tagging all over Paris. People get glimpses of her in purple but that is it. Did she talk to you?"

I shrugged, guessing we could equally be ignorant about each other. I didn't know she was famous, and she didn't know I was notorious. Maybe she had liked that as much as I had.

"You didn't have to stop for me. I'm good. I was making my way home. Go back for your run."

He looked around. "You made it about two miles. That's not bad for never running."

"Well, maybe I'm a stronger runner in my heels and a wedding dress."

Zeke stroked his hand through his hair, and I wished he were doing it to mine. "Was that just a few days ago? Feels like a lot longer."

"Well, I have that effect on people." I batted my eyes. "One minute with me feels like a lifetime. I can be too much."

"Hey." The anger in his voice surprised me. "Don't talk about yourself that way. You're a lovely human being. Amazing, really. Look at you. You're in Paris days, and you're making friends with the purple dabbler."

"I wouldn't say friends. More like we spoke on the street. Come on. Let's go."

I didn't want to think about what his complimenting me did to me, how it made me feel warm inside. It was better to hold on to the embarrassment of this morning. That way I could never make that mistake again.

"Oh no." He glared at me. "You ran here. Run home. Finish strong. Come on, I'll stay with you."

I shook my head. "That'll be agony for you. I'll give

running back a try, but you go your pace and I'll go mine. I've already humiliated myself in front of you once for the day."

Zeke rocked back on his heels. "What are you talking about?"

"When I propositioned you. I won't do that again. I only have the means to make myself look a fool twice in one week." I winked at him, which I hoped kept things jovial. "And now that I've acknowledged it, we can move on, yes?"

I ran past him, managing to not get hit as I crossed the street and headed back toward his house. By the time we got there, I was aching. My muscles just weren't used to the kind of activity I was asking of them. I was out of shape, and it was not okay. I was going to fix this. Some things I couldn't control, this I could. I had to stop.

Nearly colliding with a woman who carried groceries, including the cliché long French bread that made it really look like French groceries, I bent over to hold my knees as I gasped for air.

"You know." Zeke stopped, putting his hand on my head like he was offering support in my moment of need. "When I first ran up there, I thought you were talking to a guy. I couldn't really see who you were conversing with. I thought I might have lost you. In our pretend relationship."

I groaned. Talking was hard, but I managed. "In our pretend relationship?"

"Yes." He stretched his arms over his head, giving me a view of his stomach. Fucking beautiful man.

Okay. He wanted to play. "What if it was a man? You turned me down. Did you think I'd sit and wait for you?" I leaned forward, letting him look at my cleavage. "That's right. Take a good solid stare. None of this will ever belong to you. I changed my mind."

He tugged me to him so close, I could feel his heartbeat

against my hand, feel his breath on my face. It was warm and sweet.

"Go ahead and run, Layla. The day you pulled me into your gravitation meant that you'd never get away from me. I might turn you away a million times. But you'll always belong to me, whether I want you or not, little girl. You're mine to take or to throw away. As I see fit." He winked again. "In this pretend world we're playing in. Since in real life, I don't do relationships. Ever."

I pushed away from him. Infuriating man. I'd rather run through the pain than put up with any more than this. Damn my stupid hormones and the way I had always wanted Zeke. I had to get over this.

I'd had enough trouble for one lifetime when it came to men.

————

The café was less filled today. The weekend crowd wasn't there, and Zeke was in a good mood. He must like it when there were fewer people to contend with. This time, I didn't feel embarrassed that I couldn't talk. I'd made it through the last few days without falling on my head. I wasn't going to worry about a little thing like not being able to understand what most people here were saying.

The waitress set down the breadbasket, and this time, I grabbed a croissant without worrying about it. My hair was still damp from my shower. There was butter and jelly too. I couldn't have been happier. Zeke ordered us eggs and coffee. I smiled into my breakfast. This was a beautiful day.

Even if he made me want to smack him sometimes. Why did it make me only want him more? I was like a walking advertisement for what not to do.

Renee and Danette came in together. When they saw me,

they grinned and ran over, speaking fast in French before they remembered.

"My date was wonderful. Thank you. It's because of you."

"Me?" I shook my head. "Your date was wonderful because of you."

They liked that and took off to what had to be their regular table.

"You make friends really easily." Zeke ate his eggs slowly. "I said it before, and I meant it. You just did."

Not usually. "Do you make friends easily?"

"I've had the same three friends for years. Otherwise, I don't bother. People are acquaintances through business. Pseudo-friends."

Well, that was three more friends than I had. Although, I supposed I had my sisters. I'd been avoiding my phone. There would be time later to answer questions and see what people were saying online. It was kind of freeing to not care.

"I have people who like to be seen with me." The coffee was delicious. "What do your friends do now?"

"One of them runs a bar in New Jersey. One of them is married with two kids. He's an electrician. They live in Chicago. And one of them is constantly traveling. He wants to see the whole world. Always a wanderer, that one." He smiled while he spoke. "Howard. Seamus. And Cory. We met in foster care."

Danette rushed over to the table again. "You come with me after you finish eating, yes?"

I blinked. "Where do you want me to go?"

"Shopping." She clapped her hands together. "Come with me, please. I have two friends. We can go and meet them. We'll go shopping today."

My stomach clenched. "I don't actually think I can do that."

Her face fell, and I felt like I'd kicked a puppy.

People always wanted to shop with me. I never really wanted to, but I'd gotten used to it.

"Want to?" Zeke tilted his head.

I nodded. I wouldn't mind taking a break from how confusing he was to my emotions. I hated shopping, but at least I knew how to do it. "Can't."

Zeke reached into his pocket and pulled out a credit card before sliding it over to me. I stared at it. He'd said he would pay for me while I was here. But still I didn't want to go shopping on his dime like it was nothing at all. I took it just in case, but I wasn't going to spend money. I'd go with them, but I wouldn't buy for me. That was always fairly easy to get away with. No one really wanted to shop with me for me. It was for them. And I was glad to help.

I turned toward Zeke. "Is it okay? Honey?"

"Sure." His mouth twitched. "Danette, you have my address? You'll have her back by three? I need her tonight. So, she has to get ready." His gaze fell to me again. "Don't be gone too long, princess. I'll miss you too much if you spend the whole day away."

I wanted to roll my eyes at myself. He didn't mean it. I wasn't his princess any more than he was my honey. Even if I wished such a life could exist.

CHAPTER FOURTEEN

Danette knew all the best thrift shops in town, and she and her friend Mariana were very lively and fun. Every once in a while, Mariana and I stumbled in the language department. French wasn't her first language, she'd actually been born in Portugal and English was her third language. Considering I couldn't speak anything but English, I wasn't one to judge. I think they found me cute, despite their being two years younger than me, and we all got on just fine. By the end of the excursion, they'd bought every designer thing they spotted in the stores and really didn't need my help at all in selecting their clothing, which was good since I absolutely was not in the mood to play stylist.

I was too worked up about Zeke. By the tenth selfie the girls and I took, I was over that, too. It wasn't like I minded. I didn't have friends who didn't want to pose with me. That was just how it went. But I was cranky, sore from my run—which was getting worse by the moment—and flustered.

What did it mean that he kept kissing me and then changing his mind? Or maybe he just went around kissing lots of people. That woman from the first day in the café had certainly made it seem like he was love them and leave them.

Four days or something like that.

Maybe I should feel lucky he seemed so pseudo-disinterested. But fuck. I wasn't uninterested. I wanted his attention. I wanted to feel his hard muscles push down on me in the bed. I wanted his mouth on my nipples. I wanted to lick the sweat off his body.

I shook my head. This kind of thinking really didn't help anything. If I didn't want him to kiss me and get me all worked up, I would simply tell him to keep his hands to himself. And I would stay out of his bed to avoid any future embarrassments when my guard was down in the morning.

No more muss, no more fuss.

We were getting ready to leave the store when I stopped abruptly. It had been a long time since a shirt caught my attention the way the one in front of me did. It was a plain white T-shirt with the word *$5 Graphic Tee Shirt* across the front. I grinned. The meta-irony of that was sort of fantastic. Maybe it was kind of dumb, but it was sort of perfect in its ridiculousness. I had to have it.

I rushed over and grabbed it. I didn't own anything like it. What would I pair it with? I was going to need jeans. That was great. This place had that, too. Oh, and then there was a really cute bunch of socks with cats on them. When was the last time I had wanted to shop? Well, I'd never had the option to own clothes like this.

This stuff was cheesy, not the latest fashion, and no one was going to want to emulate me for wearing them, but I had to have this stuff. For the first time in a long while, it felt like I had found something that spoke to me. I might have finally done what people bought my book to learn, I might have found my fashion.

And it was pure, undiluted vintage cheese meshed with irony and ridiculousness. I'd never have guessed it.

Oh, there was a picture on that T-shirt of a soda that said *Don't Drink Soda* and another one that said *This Shirt Sucks*. I laughed. This was fantastic. Some of them were in French. I skipped over them. Whoever had selected their English graphic tees had really made my day.

Forget Zeke. This was fun.

Danette dropped me off outside of Zeke's house and gave me a hug. She wanted to do this again sometime, but I was done with clothes shopping for a while. I walked past the guard, waving at him, and entered the house. I wondered if there would ever come a time I didn't flinch at the downstairs. As far as I could tell, outside of the kitchen, Zeke spent almost no time there at all.

And I didn't blame him one bit. It was awful.

I carried my few bags upstairs. Zeke was yelling on the phone with someone, and I winced. That did not sound like happiness. My stomach clenched. I'd missed a meal. It really was amazing how quickly I'd adjusted to this constant eating.

Quickly—because I'd been practically giddy to put on my new clothes the whole ride home—I changed into my jeans. They had ripped holes in the knees. I was pretty sure they'd been designed that way because they were too symmetrical to be manmade. Then I put on my $5 T-shirt. It had cost the equivalent of two American dollars.

There was some sort of crazy irony in that, too. Really, I was enjoying this way too much.

I finally looked down at my phone. I had messages from my sisters. A lot of them. And one from Justin, plus one from

Kit. My stomach clenched. It was the last two that made me avoid the phone.

Unable to even open the app to see what they said, I scrolled through my social media presence instead. There I was. Kissing Zeke on the dance floor. Great. He'd be getting what he wanted. My father had to be hearing about this and reacting soon. If he hadn't already. Maybe that was why Zeke was yelling.

I put on my sneakers and braided my hair into two long braids à la Heidi because I felt like it and it let me avoid my messages for a few minutes later. Lip gloss seemed to complete the outfit, so I put some on, too.

With a sigh, I finally looked at what had been sent to me.

You're making out with Zeke! That was Hope. She messaged a few minutes later. *Holy. Fucking. Shit. I mean...Layla, I am speechless.*

I grinned and texted her back. *Long story, but yes, I am making out with him.* There was more to say, and I'd say it later when this little experiment to get under my father's skin was over. Then she could hear the whole frustrating tale.

Bridget was next. *Layla! You're dating Zeke? I saw your post. Be careful with him. He's not an easy person. I think he has a secret history.* Well, she was right about that. Mom killed herself, lived in foster care. He did some things to survive he'd probably not like to talk about, except apparently with me. *Although, if anyone could bring someone's heart around, it would be you. You always were the most loving and kindest of all of us.*

I stared at her words. Hope was usually the one to talk about emotions. But Bridget had it wrong. Hope was the one who was the kindest and most overtly loving. I was always a little bit lost.

Not true. I texted her back. *Most days I don't know which way is up with emotions. I just left my fiancé at the altar.*

With my back steeled, I played with one of my braids and forced myself to look at Justin's message.

I hate you.

That was all it said. He hated me. Rage surged through me before I forced myself to cool it down. He hated me? What on Earth could I have done to have earned that? I didn't do anything to him.

I flipped over to the message from Kit and groaned. He had a woman naked beneath him. And beneath the picture were the words *you're a slut.*

For half a second, I wondered who had taken that photo, but then it quickly moved on to more important things. I was a slut and my brother hated me.

I threw my phone down on the bed so hard it bounced into the air before hitting my pillow. Maybe I should have done it harder and let it crack on the floor. Then no one could contact me at all.

I left the room before I could overthink it and went to the kitchen. There had to be food. I wasn't eating for hours. Zeke hadn't told me that, but this was France, they ate later than Americans. I needed something to tide me over. Not eating wasn't going to happen on the days that I ran.

And yes, I planned to do it again. Even hated sluts could run to take care of their stress.

I opened the fridge. A plate was wrapped, and I took it out, knowing immediately it wasn't for me. It was a salad with chicken the chef had made for Zeke. How did I know? It was very specific. Dressing on the side, chicken cooked until it was blackened. It didn't look like something made for me.

He hadn't eaten lunch.

Well...that wasn't good. A hungry Zeke was going to be even more unpleasant than a well-fed Zeke. I set his plate down on the counter and grabbed some cheese and meat I found in a drawer. He really liked cheese. Cutting off a bit for myself, I ate mine with some crackers quickly before I downed some water. That was enough food. I was hungry, but that didn't mean I had to overeat.

I grabbed some of the cheese for Zeke, put it on another plate, and poured him the last of a wine he'd corked in the fridge. On quiet feet, I headed upstairs and knocked on his door.

"What?" he yelled in response, and I cracked it open.

Before he could holler at me to go away, I held up the plates and glass I was doing a rather poor job of balancing. I was, however, determined not to spill. "Brought your lunch."

He sat at his desk staring at me for a long second before he nodded. "Thanks. You didn't have to do that."

"I know. But I wanted to." I smiled again and set it down on a clear portion of his desk. "See you later."

I would have left, but he stopped me with his words. "You look really, really pretty. When did you get that? Or is it something you brought with you?"

Damn it. He'd made me flutter inside. "I got it today. I used your card. But it was cheap. I could pay you back, probably."

"Don't." He took a bite of the salad and then stared at the cheese. "Did Henry give me this cheese?"

"No, that was me. I know you really like cheese, and I thought it might make the salad more exciting."

He took a large bite. "You've made my day. You have no idea. How was the shopping?"

"It was good, actually. I got some things I love." I headed toward his door. "Enjoy your lunch. Oh, we're all over social media so there must be some kind of response coming. If my dad is going to screw up, it must be coming. That kiss from last night was genius."

He set down his fork. "What?"

"The kiss. On the dance floor. You clearly did it for the

cameras. We're everywhere. So good work." Look at me being breezy and acting like I didn't care.

A muscle ticked in his jaw. "I didn't kiss you for some cameras. Is that what you think?"

No, it hadn't been until he'd turned me down this morning. I shrugged. Lightweight and easy going. That was the name of the game. "See you later, Zeke."

I left him sitting there and closed the door behind me. I didn't know what game I was playing or even what the rules were, but I'd just scored points if, for no other reason, I'd let him think I could care about nothing, too. When this was over, and I went on to whatever was next, I'd have the ability to pretend better than I ever had before. And that had to count for something.

I went back to my room and climbed onto the bed.

There were more messages. Hope and Bridget had both answered, and of course one more for Justin. The truth was that I deserved Kit's anger. Maybe I'd been wrong in assuming his feelings for me were as negative as mine were for him. Maybe I had hurt him a lot. I'd embarrassed him, that was for sure. But it wasn't like he'd come to find me and ask me what had happened. It wasn't as though he'd begged me to give us another chance.

I'd take his abuse. I deserved it. However, Justin was a mystery. Why was he doing this to me?

You've always thought you were better than the rest of us.

I laughed, but it wasn't from amusement. I wasn't better than anyone. I was just the opposite. The one who couldn't find her way, even with pointed directions.

I lay down on the bed. Was gravity somehow suddenly stronger?

It felt like it was going to push me over, keep me from being upright ever again. I rolled over and pressed my face into the pillow. I'd just stay like this until I had to get beautiful for dinner again.

That was my role in life after all.

A knock sounded, and the door opened before I could say come in. What was the point of knocking? I managed to roll over to see Zeke standing in the door frame.

"I want to talk about what you just said."

I groaned. "Okay."

"I..." His voice trailed off. "What's wrong?"

"Nothing." I grabbed the pillow and covered my face with it. So much for my little win a minute ago. He was going to lay into me now, and I was going to take it because I didn't want to go back to New York yet. Those were my choices. Here. Or New York.

The bed sagged where he must have sat down on it next to me. "Layla?"

I moved the pillow. "My brother."

"What about him?" Zeke's voice was hard. "What is he doing to you? He's already abandoned you in Paris, leaving you penniless after stealing from you."

I wanted to groan again, but that wasn't an answer. Instead, I handed him my phone. He could see all the things that everyone sent me and that was fine. I had no secrets. Nothing I was saying to Hope or Bridget was anything I shouldn't. I was keeping our deal just fine.

He stared at it for a second, looking at Justin's message, his jaw hardening while he did. A second or two later he swiped his finger over it, and I had no idea who he was looking at now. I closed my eyes. Let him have at my phone.

"Just give me a few minutes to collect myself, and then I'll start to get pretty enough to go to dinner. I need to put this away wherever I shove these things inside of me for my future nervous breakdown."

He was so quiet, I wondered if I'd imagined him being there to begin with. "Layla."

I forced my eyes open, braced for this to get worse. "Go for it. Whatever you need to say, say it."

"I'm sorry your brother is so sick. And I'm sorry that he's taking it out on you. My mother, who killed herself, was an addict. I mean, I didn't understand that at the time, but I figured it out eventually when I reexamined things. I don't think... I mean, I don't think this is Justin in his right mind. I knew him a little bit years ago when he interned at the company. He was a nice guy. This seems like...like it's the illness, the addiction, the drugs, not Justin."

I didn't know my brother well enough to make that statement. "I've never... He and I aren't close. We never have been. And he's very preoccupied with sending me mean messages."

Zeke sighed and lay back on the bed next to me. "Probably because he feels guilty. He knows what he did. And he's redirecting it right back onto you. Now Kit, on the other hand? I could take care of this problem for you."

I laughed. "I would think you were past the I'll-beat-up-your-ex phase of life."

"I'm not going to beat him up. I'm going to have someone find him and make it stop."

I shook my head. "As for Kit, I think he gets to do this for a little bit. He gets to hurt me if he wants to."

"No, sweetheart, he doesn't." He rolled over to look at me. "Don't change your clothes. We'll go somewhere else for dinner. Some place where you can stay right as you are. I love it." He tugged on the end of my braid. "It's somehow...very you."

"That's how I felt about it. Jeans and a T-shirt. Who would have thought it? I can have any clothes in the world, and this is all I want to wear from now and forever." I shrugged. "Or maybe just for today."

He smoothed his thumb over my bottom lip. "I didn't kiss you for the cameras. I forgot that was a possibility in that moment. Oh, but before I forget, I did talk to your publisher today. He is emailing you five ideas for you to write a book about. Or collaborate on one. However you want to do it. They'd love to have you back."

I nodded. That made sense. I supposed. That was what I had done to make a living in the past, and maybe I could make that work again. "Thanks."

"You're welcome. That's the deal, right. You help me, I help you."

I put out my hand. "Put her there, partner."

He took my outstretched offering, but he brought it to his mouth and kissed it. "We'll take my motorcycle to dinner."

"Then you can't drink. That's no fun for you."

"Looking at you across the table is plenty fun, gorgeous."

I rolled my eyes at him. That was a line if I ever heard one. "Whatever you want."

He stroked my hair off my face. "Layla, in all seriousness, you haven't done anything to deserve that kind of hate from your brother. I like that his texts are what bother you and not that scumbag Kit. But you don't deserve his either. If I had a fiancée and she ran from the altar, I would chase her. I would at least find out why and try to fix what had terrified her. He ran off with your brother and left you to fend for yourself. Not that I should be talking. I'm never getting married, so I won't have that problem."

"I'm going to adopt your philosophy in life. I'm going to decide that I'm simply not getting married and be done with the whole thing."

He snorted, which was a funny noise coming from him.

"You are entirely the type of person to fall in love and get married forever. You are made for that."

"Don't presume to know me just because we've spent a few days together now."

"Ah, I see." Zeke ran his finger over my knuckles. "You have a side to you I have yet to see, is that it? I'm reading you wrong."

Truth was he probably wasn't. "No, you're right. I pretty much am what I am."

"There's not a thing wrong with that. I like who you are. You should like you, too." He rose from the bed. "I'm going to go back to work."

I leaned up on my elbows to regard him before he left. "Maybe when this is over, you could introduce me to men." I didn't know why I was needling him. "The kind that I should meet and marry. Maybe you could make me a list."

The look he shot me could burn me to ash if he had laser eyes. "See you later, Layla."

He would. We were going to have dinner, and I'd try to solve the enigma he was while I still had the ability to do so. Surely my father should be making his error soon. And it looked like I had a career if my publisher wanted me back.

All of our issues had been handled. No more problems.

If only life worked like that. The truth was it was as though I was sort of on sabbatical from reality, hanging out with Zeke before I went back to my real life in New York. I rose from the bed and looked at the desk on the other side of the room. He really had it decorated like a hotel. There was even a small blank packet of paper and a pencil inside of it.

I picked it up, the need to draw coming over me more strongly than it had in a long time. Most of the time, I ignored the need to do any kind of artwork. My father didn't approve of it. He didn't want us to be our mother, and considering things, I thought he was probably right. I was the most like her. My sisters were sensible. They knew how to navigate their lives without these kinds of problems.

The Banksy of Paris had caught my attention earlier. I started to sketch my mom's face. I couldn't remember her, but there was one picture of her that traveled with us everywhere when we moved. It was always placed in our bedroom, as if that would offer us some kind of comfort. Maybe it did for my sisters. We never discussed it amongst ourselves. For me, it creeped me out. My dead mother staring at me, forever twenty-two, smiling at something someone said to her off the camera. Her eyes were bright, her smile huge. The epitome of womanhood to me for so many years.

What if I didn't want to smile?

I rubbed my eyes. I was overthinking this. I should stop this nonsense and check my email to see what they suggested I should write for them. I could look at Instagram and see what was happening to my image. But I didn't. I sketched her. Like she looked in that picture but different. No one would really understand what I was doing. I changed her eyes. They were triangles, not real.

Smirking, I kept going. Look at me being ridiculous like I could make abstract art. So stupid, my father would say to me. Why are you wasting your time? You're not an artist, Layla. You're a joke. What are the chances you could be any kind of success like she was in her short years? They'd only ever see you as a secondary choice to her and not a very good one.

You know what, Dad? Go fuck yourself from my thoughts. You don't get to take up any more space in my head without paying rent for your time there. We can pay off my wedding with the money you owe me for existing in my subconscious.

I was going to draw, and there wasn't a thing my dad— there or not—could do about it anymore.

I'd gone through three quarters of my paper when a knock sounded again. "Come in."

I didn't look up.

"Layla?"

Zeke's voice flooded the room, and it forced my attention off my paper. "Oh, sorry. I…I lost track of time."

"Do you want to watch the sunset with me?" He strolled over to the bed and stared down at my discarded papers, picking one up. It was a version of my mother, where I'd made her stop smiling. "I thought you didn't draw."

"Before today, I didn't."

And that was so strange, I loved it.